THE MAN WHO DI

(AND THREE OTHERS)

MORE WILDSIDE CLASSICS

Please see www.wildsidepress.com for a complete list!

THE MAN WHO DIED TWICE
(AND THREE OTHERS)

FRANK BELKNAP LONG

WILDSIDE PRESS

THE MAN WHO DIED TWICE (AND THREE OTHERS)

This edition published in 2009 by Wildside Press, LLC.
www.wildsidebooks.com

"The Man Who Died Twice" originally appeared in *Ghost Stories*, January 1927. "Humpty Dumpty had a Great Fall" originally appeared in *Startling Stories*, November 1948. "The Sky Trap" originally appeared in *Comet*, July 1941. "The Mississippi Saucer" originally appeared in *Weird Tales*, March 1951.

CONTENTS

THE MAN WHO DIED TWICE

WHEN Hazlitt saw the stranger at his desk his emotions were distinctly unpleasant. "Upcher might have given me notice," he thought. "He wouldn't have been so high-handed a few months ago!"

He gazed angrily about the office. No one seemed aware of his presence. The man who had taken his desk was dictating a letter, and the stenographer did not even raise her eyes. "It's damnable!" said Hazlitt, and he spoke loud enough for the usurper to hear; but the latter continued to dictate: "The premium on policy 6284 has been so long overdue—"

Hazlitt stalked furiously across the office and stepped into a room blazing with light and clamorous with conversation. Upcher, the President, was in conference, but Hazlitt ignored the three directors who sat puffing contentedly on fat cigars, and addressed himself directly to the man at the head of the table.

"I've worked for you for twenty years," he shouted furiously, "and you needn't think you can dish me now. I've helped make this company. If necessary, I shall take legal steps—"

Mr. Upcher was stout and stern. His narrow skull and small eyes under heavy eyebrows, suggested a very primitive type. He had stopped talking and was staring directly at Hazlitt. His gaze was icily indifferent—stony, remote. His calm was so unexpected that it frightened Hazlitt.

The directors seemed perplexed. Two of them had stopped smoking, and the third was passing his hand rapidly back and forth across his forehead. "I've frightened them," thought Hazlitt. "They know the old man owes everything to me. I mustn't appear too submissive."

"You can't dispose of me like this," he continued dogmatically. "I've never complained of the miserable salary you gave me, but you can't throw me into the street without notice."

The President colored slightly. "Our business is very important—" he began.

Hazlitt cut him short with a wave of his hand. "My business is the only thing that matters now. . . . I want you to know that I won't stand for your ruthless tactics. When a man has slaved as I have for twenty years he deserves some consideration. I am merely asking for justice. In heaven's name, why don't you say something? Do you want me to do all of the talking?"

Mr. Upcher wiped away with his coat sleeve the small beads of sweat that had accumulated above his collar. His gaze remained curiously impersonal, and when Hazlitt swore at him he wet his lips and began: "Our business is very important—"

Hazlitt trembled at the repetition of the man's unctuous remark. He found himself reluctant to say more, but his anger continued to mount. He advanced threateningly to the head of the table and glared into the impassive eyes of his former employer. Finally he broke out: "You're a damn scoundrel!"

One of the directors coughed. A sickly grin spread itself across Mr. Upcher's stolid countenance. "Our business, as I was saying—"

Hazlitt raised his fist and struck the president of the Richbank Life Insurance Company squarely upon the jaw. It was an intolerably ridiculous thing to do, but Hazlitt was no longer capable of verbal persuasion. And he had decided that nothing less than a blow would be adequate.

The grin disappeared from Mr. Upcher's face. He raised his right hand and passed it rapidly over his chin. A flash of anger appeared for a moment in

his small, deep-set eyes. "Something I don't understand," he murmured. "It hurt like the devil. I don't know precisely what it means!"

"Don't you?" shouted Hazlitt. "You're lucky to get off with that. I've a good mind to hit you again." But he was frightened at his own violence, and he was unable to understand why the directors had not seized him. They seemed utterly unaware of anything out of the ordinary: and even Mr. Upcher did not seem greatly upset. He continued to rub his chin, but the old indifference had crept back into his eyes.

"Our business is very important—" he began.

"Policies that have been carried for more than fifty years," he was saying, "are not subject to the new law. It is possible by the contemplated—"

Hazlitt did not wait for him to finish. Sobbing hysterically he passed into the outer office, and several minutes later he was descending in the elevator to the street. All moral courage had left him; he felt like a man who has returned from the grave. He was white to the lips, and when he

Hazlitt broke down and wept. He leaned against the wall while great sobs convulsed his body. Anger and abuse he could have faced, but Mr. Upcher's stony indifference robbed him of manhood. It was impossible to argue with a man who refused to be insulted. Hazlitt had reached the end of his rope; he was decisively beaten. But even his acknowledgment of defeat passed unnoticed. The directors were discussing policies and premiums and first mortgages, and Mr. Upcher advanced a few commonplace opinions while his right hand continued to caress his chin.

stopped for a moment in the vestibule he was horrified at the way an old woman poked at him with her umbrella and actually pushed him aside.

The glitter and chaos of Broadway at dusk did not soothe him. He walked despondently, with his hands in his pockets and his eyes upon the ground. "I'll never get another job," he thought. "I'm a nervous wreck and old Upcher will never

recommend me. I don't know how I'll break the news to Helen."

The thought of his wife appalled him. He knew that she would despise him. "She'll think I'm a jellyfish," he groaned. "But I did all a man could. You can't buck up against a stone wall. I can see that old Upcher had it in for me from the start. I hope he chokes!"

He crossed the street at 73rd Street and started leisurely westward. It was growing dark and he stopped for a moment to look at his watch. His hands trembled and the timepiece almost fell to the. sidewalk. With an oath he replaced it in his vest. "Dinner will be cold," he muttered. "And Helen won't be in a pleasant mood. How on earth am I going to break the news to her?"

WHEN he reached his apartment he was shivering. He sustained himself by tugging at the ends of his mustache and whistling apologetically. He was overcome with shame and fear but something urged him not to put off ringing the bell.

He pressed the buzzer firmly, but no reassuring click answered him. Yet—suddenly he found himself in his own apartment. "I certainly got in," he mumbled in an immeasurably frightened voice, "but I apparently didn't come through the door . . . or did I? I don't think I'm quite well."

He hung up his hat and umbrella, and walked into the sitting room. His wife was perched on the arm of his Morris chair, and her back was turned towards him. She was in dressing gown and slippers, and her hair was down. She was whispering in a very low voice: "My dear; my darling! I hope you haven't worked too hard today. You must take care of your health for my sake. Poor Richard went off in three days with double pneumonia.

Hazlitt stared. The woman on the chair was obviously not addressing him, and he thought for an instant that he had strayed into the wrong apartment and mistaken a stranger for his wife. But the familiar lines of her profile soon undeceived him, and he gasped. Then in a blinding flash he saw it all. His wife had betrayed him, and she was speaking to another man.

Hazlitt quickly made up his mind that he would kill his wife. He advanced ominously to where she sat, and stared at her with furious, bloodshot eyes. She shivered and glanced about her nervously. The stranger in the chair rose and stood with his back to the fireplace. Hazlitt saw that he was tall and lean, and handsome. He seemed happy, and was smiling.

Hazlitt clenched his fist and glared fiercely at this intruder into his private home.

"Something has come between us," said Hazlitt's wife in a curiously distant voice. "I feel it like a physical presence. You will perhaps think me very silly."

The stranger shook his head. "I feel it too," he said. "It's as if the ghost of an old love had come back to you. While you were sitting on the chair I saw a change come over your face. I think you fear something."

"I'll make you both fear something!" shouted Hazlitt. He struck his wife on the face with his open hand. She colored slightly and continued to address the stranger. "It's as if *he* had come back. It is six months tonight since we buried him. He was a good husband and I am not sure that I have reverenced his memory. Perhaps we were too hasty, Jack!"

Hazlitt suppressed an absurd desire to scream. The blood was pounding in his ears, and he gazed from his wife to the stranger with stark horror. His wife's voice sent a flood of dreadful memories welling through his consciousness.

He saw again the hospital ward where he had spent three days of terrible agony, gasping for breath and shrieking for water. A tall doctor with sallow bloodless cheeks bent wearily above him and injected something into his arm. Then unconsciousness, a blessed oblivion wiping out the world and all its disturbing sights and sounds.

Later he opened his eyes and caught his wife in the act of poisoning him. He saw her standing above him with a spoon, and a bottle in her hand, on which was a skull and crossbones. He endeavored to rise up, to cry out, but his voice failed him and he could not move his limbs. He saw that his wife was possessed of a devil and primitive horror fastened on his tired brain.

He made dreadful grimaces and squirmed about under the sheets, but his wife was relentless. She bent and forced the spoon between his teeth. "I don't love you," she laughed shrilly. "And you're better dead. I only hope you won't return to haunt me!"

Hazlitt choked and fainted. He did not regain consciousness but later he watched his body being prepared for burial, and amused himself by thinking that his wife would soon regret her vileness. "I shall show her what a ghost can do!" he reflected grimly. "I shall pay her for this! She won't love me when I'm through with her!"

There had followed days of confusion. Hazlitt forgot that he was only a ghost, and he had walked into his old office and deliberately insulted Mr. Upcher. But now that his wife stood before him memories came rushing back. He was a thin, emaciated ghost, but he could make himself felt.

Nothing but vengeance remained to him, and he did not intend to forgive his wife. It was not in his nature to forgive. He would force a confession from her, and if necessary he would choke the breath from her abominable body. He advanced and seized her by the throat.

He was pressing with all his might upon the delicate white throat of his wife. He was pressing with lean, bony fingers; his victim seemed sunk into a kind of stupor. Her eyes were half-shut and she was leaning against the wall.

THE stranger watched her with growing horror. When she began to cough he ran into the kitchen and returned with a glass of water. When he handed it to her she drained it at a gulp. It seemed to restore her slightly. "I can't explain it," she murmured. "But I feel as if a band were encircling my throat. It is hot in here. Please open the windows!"

The stranger obeyed. It occurred to Hazlitt that the man really loved his wife. "Worse luck to him!" he growled, and his ghostly voice cracked with emotion. The woman was choking and gasping now and gradually he forced her to her knees.

"Confess," he commanded. "Tell this fool how you get rid of your husbands. Warn him in advance, and he will thank you and clear out. If you love him you won't want him to suffer."

Hazlitt's wife made no sign that she had heard him. "You're doing no good at all by acting like this!" he shouted, "If you don't tell him everything now I'll kill you! I'll make you a ghost!"

The tall stranger turned pale. He could not see or hear Hazlitt but it was obvious that he suspected the presence of more than two people in the room. He took Hazlitt's wife firmly by the wrists and endeavored to raise her.

"In heaven's name what ails you?" he asked fearfully. You act as if someone were hurting you. Is there nothing that I can do?"

There was something infinitely pathetic in the woman's helplessness. She was no longer able to speak, but her eyes cried out in pain. . . . The stranger at length succeeded in aiding her. He got her to her feet, but Hazlitt refused to be discouraged. The stranger's opposition exasperated him and he redoubled his efforts. But soon he realized that he could not choke her. He had expended all his strength and still the woman breathed. A convulsion of baffled rage distorted his angular frame. He knew that he would be obliged to go away and leave the woman to her lover. A ghost is a futile thing at best and cannot work vengeance. Hazlitt groaned.

The woman beneath his hands took courage. Her eyes sought those of the tall stranger. "It is going away; it is leaving me," she whimpered. "I can breathe more easily now. It is you who have given me courage, my darling."

The stranger was bewildered and horrified. "I can't understand what's got into you," he murmured. "I don't see anything. You are becoming hysterical. Your nerves are all shattered to pieces."

Hazlitt's wife shook her head and color returned to her cheeks. "It was awful, dearest. You cannot know how I suffered.

You will perhaps think me insane, but I know he was back of it. Kiss me darling; help me to forget." She threw her arms about the stranger's neck and kissed him passionately upon the lips.

Hazlitt covered his eyes with his hand and turned away with horror. Despair clutched at his heart. "A futile ghost," he groaned. "A futile, weak ghost! I couldn't punish a fly. Why in heaven's name am I earthbound?"

He was near the window now, and suddenly he looked out. A night of stars attracted him. "I shall climb to heaven," he thought. "I shall go floating through the air, and wander among the stars. I am decidedly out of place here."

IT was a tired ghost that climbed out of the window, and started to propel itself through the air. But unfortunately a man must overcome gravitation to climb to the stars, and Hazlitt did not ascend. He was still earthbound.

He picked himself up and looked about him. Men and women were passing rapidly up and down the street but no one had apparently seen him fall.

"I'm invisible, that's sure," he reflected. "Neither Upcher, nor the directors nor my wife saw me. But my wife felt me. And yet I'm not satisfied. I didn't accomplish what I set out to do. My wife is laughing up her sleeve at me now. My wife? She has probably married that ninny, and I hope she lives to regret it. She didn't even wait for the grass to cover my grave. I won't trust a woman again if I can help it."

A woman walking on the street passed through him. "Horrible!" he groaned. "There isn't anything to me at all! I'm worse than a jellyfish!"

An entire procession of men and women were now passing through his invisible body. He scarcely felt them, but a few succeeded in tickling him. One or two of the pedestrians apparently felt him: they shivered as if they had suddenly stepped into a cold shower.

"The streets are ghostly at night," someone said at his left elbow, "I think it's safer to ride."

Hazlitt determined to walk. He was miserable, but he had no desire to stand and mope. He started down the street. He was hatless and his hair streamed in the wind. He was a defiant ghost, but a miserable sense of futility gripped him. He was an outcast. He did not know where he would spend the night. He had no plans and no one to confide in. He couldn't go to a hotel because he hadn't even the ghost of money in his pockets, and of course no one could see him anyway.

Suddenly he saw a child standing in the very center of the street, and apparently unaware of the screaming traffic about him. An automobile driven by a young woman was almost on top of the boy before Hazlitt made up his mind to act.

He left the sidewalk in a bound and ran directly towards the automobile. He reached it a second before it touched the child, and with a great shove he sent the near-victim sprawling into a zone of safety. But he could not save himself. The fender of the car struck him violently in the chest; he was thrown forward, and the rear wheels passed over his body.

For a moment he suffered exquisite pain; a great weight pressed the breath from his thin body. He clenched his hands, and closed his eyes. The pain of this second death astonished him; it seemed interminable. But at length consciousness left him; his pain dissolved in a healing oblivion.

THE child picked himself up and began to cry. "Someone pushed me," he moaned. "I was looking at the lights and someone pushed me from behind."

The woman in the car was very pale. "I think I ran over someone," she said weakly. "I saw him for a moment when I tried to turn to the left. He was very thin and worn." She turned to those who had gathered near. "Where did you carry him to?" she asked.

They shook their heads. "We didn't see anyone, madam! You nearly got the kid though. Drivers like you should be hanged!"

A policeman roughly elbowed his way through the crowd that was fast gathering: "What's all this about?" he asked. "Is anyone run over?"

The woman shook her head. "I don't know. I think I ran over a tramp . . . a poor, thin man he was . . . the look in his eyes was terrible . . . and very beautiful. I . . . I saw him for a moment just before the car struck him. I think he wanted to die."

She turned again to the crowd. "Which of you carried him away?" she asked tremulously.

"She's batty," said the policeman. "Get out of here you!" He advanced on the crowd and began dispersing them with his club.

The woman in the car leaned over and looked at the sidewalk, a puzzled, mystified expression on her pale features.

"No blood or anything," she moaned. "I can't understand it!"

HUMPTY DUMPTY
HAD A GREAT FALL

Kenneth Wayne was dressing for dinner when he heard the tapping. It was loud, insistent, and seemed to be saying: "No use pretending you're not at home, old man! I can hear you moving around in there!"

Wayne groaned. He had no desire to discuss vasomotor psychology with young Graham or polytonal music with the long-haired Dr. Raydel. He was dining out with a charming girl, and he wanted to stay alive, vital, every nerve alert to her beauty.

Wayne was one of those imaginative young men who attract ideas to themselves in the fashion of a baby specialist. Instead of babies, people brought him their budding ideas to admire.

Wayne told himself that he was a fool to be annoyed. The mere sight of his tux draped across a chair should discourage a talkative visitor. With an angry shrug he turned and crossed the room in three long strides. He threw the door wide.

The boy who stood in the doorway was a stranger to him. Boy? Well, it was hard not to think of the youngster as a man, for he was heavily bearded, and he carried himself with an air of maturity. But Wayne could see that he wasn't more that eighteen or nineteen years old. His clear blue eyes held the tortured look of the very young, and there was a newness about him which contrasted sharply with Wayne's aspect of world-weariness and cynicism. Wayne was only twenty-seven, but his age rested heavily upon him. His eyes were shadowed and the planes of his face craggy with thought.

"I'm Phillip Orban," the boy said. "I ran away. They were torturing me with their questions."

The Orban boy! Wayne shut his eyes while the universe reeled. Young Orban was carrying an enormous glowing loop of hollow metal. Before Wayne could cry out in protest the trembling lad had stepped into the room and set the loop down on the floor.

"Shut the door," Orban pleaded. "Lock it tight! If they try to get in, tell them I'm not in this room."

Mechanically, Wayne locked the door. When he turned, his lips were white.

"Why did you come here?" he demanded. "Do you realize I never saw you before in my life?"

The Orban boy nodded. "I hid in a cellar under an empty house. But I was cold and hungry. I had to come out. A policeman saw me, and I had to run for it. I never saw you before, but I like you. You will tell them I'm not here?"

Wayne made a despairing gesture. "All right!" he cried. "Did I say I wouldn't? Just take it easy now. Relax!"

It seemed to Wayne that standing before him was an impossible little gnome with a conical cap on his head, made visible by a dimensional vortex that was about to dissolve in a blaze of light.

That was absurd, of course! The Orban boy wasn't one of those mutant supermen freaks science-fiction writers were always speculating about. He was a quite normal youngster who had been trapped from infancy in the mind-numbing blackness of space.

But what would be the penalty for sheltering a boy with a price on his head, a boy about whom five million words had been written? Young Orban had committed a serious crime. An ugly crime! To get rid of a man by making him disappear was not a whit less ugly than cold-blooded murder!

Wayne stared down at the shining loop of metal, his eyes wide and incredulous. "Is that the machine you built?" he demanded, and was astonished that he could speak at all.

"It's the *door* I built!" Orban said. "I didn't push Dr. Bryce into it. He stumbled and fell."

"But how did you build it?" Wayne prodded. "You never saw a tool."

"There were tools in my father's workshop," Orban said quickly. "I knew how to build it. Dr. Bryce isn't dead. He's alive in the blue world."

Structurally the machine was an incredibly simple thing. It consisted of a single loop of hollow metal, twisted into a perfect arch like a gigantic croquet wicket. It was easy to see that the loop was hollow, for it was riddled with holes, and an eerie radiance was spilling out of it.

"You've got to help me hide it," Orban pleaded. "If I don't get Dr. Bryce out of the blue, bowmen will kill him!"

Wayne turned and gripped the lad's shoulder. "You said you were hungry. Perhaps we can do something about that."

"I am hungry," the lad admitted. "But there's food in the blue world."

Wayne thought that over for a minute, then found himself propelling his guest toward the kitchen.

He left him devouring a glass of milk. No, you didn't devour milk. But the Orban boy was dipping crackers in the milk and eating the crackers. It amounted to the same thing.

Wayne felt that he needed the support of cold print. Actual confirmation of the Orban story in black type. He found the clipping by turning out all the drawers of his desk and then looking under the blotter. It was crumpled and stained, as though someone had wept bitter tears over it. It read:

THE ORBAN STORY
by Ruth Stevens

An infant rocked from birth in a cradle two hundred feet long! A little boy lost in a high-test rocketship, seesawing through space! Around and around he whirled, obeying instructions from the age of eight, eating just enough to keep the spark of life from going out.

No disease germs bothered him out there in space! There were no measles, whooping cough, scarlet fever, just instructions in his head and—a long forgetting!

What did he think about all those years? What did he dream about?

Phillip Orban was born on that ship. His father invented the Orban drive and built the first rocketship with an outer hull of sufficient hardness to withstand the stresses of a billion-mile journey through space.

But the power drive gave out, and the ship never completed its journey. It went into a circular orbit in the Asteroid Belt, and for seventeen years it drifted through space.

The boy's mother died when he was three, mercifully from a heart attack. The boy's father kept a log. We know that he climbed out on the naked hull when the boy was eight, to tighten a loosened gravity plate. A minor repair job—but he put off coming back. Put it off forever!

The boy remembered to remember. Food concentrates should be taken sparingly, twice a day. "You're seven now, son! No—eight tomorrow! Old enough to look after yourself!"

He hadn't one bittersweet, earthy moment to cling to.

He'd never played pranks on other kids, or dressed up on Halloween, or gone fishing in a creek. He'd never watched the dawn redden a haystack or the moon silver the sea.

There were books on that ship. An odd assortment of books. *The Old English Nursery Rhymes, Mother Goose,* the Brothers Grimm, Lewis Carroll. And "How to Build It" books. How to build it if you were Michael Faraday or Edison or Steinmetz or Mullson. But Phillip Orban read every book on that ship. The psychologists who are in charge of him now won't tell us why they're so excited about his marginal notes.

They found the ship and Orban at last, sank magnetic grappling irons in the hull, and towed it back to earth. They returned Orban to his home in North Dakota, the family home, within a dozen yards of his father's dust-choked workshop.

A boy of seventeen, watched night and day by three trained psychologists. A robust boy, physically almost a man, would have to be terribly warped not to resent that! They're studying him like a guinea pig in a cage. And here's one unladylike journalist who raises her voice in protest! If the Orban boy—

Wayne shuddered, folded the clipping, and crammed it in his vest pocket.

Kenneth Wayne began remembering things: about a machine in an open field spilling an eerie radiance! And Dr. Bryce struggling with the Orban boy in front of the machine and plunging backward into the light. What shocking, incredible event had taken the famed psychologist from the sunlight before he could regain his balance?

Wayne also remembered that the Orban boy had fled, taking the machine with him! A hue and cry had been raised in the nation's press. A shrill screaming, journalism raised to high C. Had Orban deliberately pushed Dr. Bryce into the machine?

If an individual were the sum total of his experiences from birth, would not the whole outlook of Orban depart from the human norm? It was a terrifying thought! Was Orban a malicious monster with an inhuman capacity for deceit? Was he—

Twang!

Wayne wheeled with a gasp of horror.

A barbed and deadly looking arrow was quivering in the wall

directly opposite the machine! It was an arrow two feet in length—fitted with metallic feathers to give it steadiness of flight and tipped with a point of jeweled brightness, visible through the translucent plastic of the wall.

Stark terror twisted Wayne's features into a glazed, unnatural mask. That the arrow had come out of the machine he could not doubt. It was directly in line with the "croquet wicket," and there was a spattering of blood on the still-quivering shaft.

There was blood on the wall too! Yet Wayne was quite sure that the arrow hadn't grazed his flesh. Automatically he raised one hand to his cheek and then stared at his palm. His hand gleamed whitely in the cold light. That dripping redness had come out of the machine along with the arrow! The arrow had missed him completely.

Whom had it wounded?

Wayne was swaying in sick horror when a knock sounded on the door and a familiar voice said:

"Ken! For heaven's sake, why did you lock the door?"

Wayne turned, unlocked the door, and threw it open, his face white.

The girl who came into the room was vividly alive. Coppery hair she had, cut in a bang, and her lips were slightly parted, her cheeks flushed. She was plainly out of breath and a little angry to be barred by a locked door after climbing two flights of stairs.

Ruth Stevens did not look like a newspaperwoman. She was striking in a challenging, vibrant way—the kind of girl who could change a man's center of gravity with a look, a quick smile.

She wasn't smiling now. Her eyes darted to the machine and then to the arrow.

"The Orban boy," Wayne said. His voice was thick, and it trembled a little, as though he were just about to lose control of it. "He's here. You wrote an article about him, remember? Would you like to meet him?"

Ruth swayed.

Wayne thought perhaps she was going to faint. It was a crazy thing to do, but he leaped toward her without realizing that he was standing a yard from the machine.

As he caught her in his arms, something caught him. It was like a fierce rush of wind. It was cyclonic. It whirled him around and started pulling him backward, straight toward the machine.

He held on to the girl without realizing that he was pulling her inexorably in the same direction.

Ruth screamed.

The room seemed to pinwheel. It was much easier for Wayne not to let go of the girl. He did not realize that she was in deadly danger. He thought only of protecting her. There was a howling in the room as light blazed out from the croquet wicket to envelop them.

Far off, as though in an inverted lens, Wayne saw the Orban boy rushing out of the kitchen, his bearded face twitching in terror. Then everything in the room seemed to whip away into emptiness. . . .

Stability came back in slow stages. Wayne was aware first of warmth in his arms, a cry quavering from human lips. Then of a firm surface taking shape beneath him.

He was sitting on the ground holding Ruth in his arms. She was struggling to free herself, one hand pushing against his chin, her face a blob of whiteness.

He was sitting with his back against a firm stone surface, staring down at her. He could see her face clearly now, distinct and white in a blue glimmering light.

"Ken, where are we?" she choked.

It wasn't an easy question to answer. It was a world of rugged contours. They seemed to be resting on a plain that sloped away into glowing blue mist. There was a curious, dynamic quality about the landscape. Its very emptiness thrust itself on Wayne like chords of music struck wildly on a piano.

Certainly he was resting with his back against a stone wall of some sort rising sheer behind him. When he turned his head, he could see the wall clearly.

With a little groan, Ruth disentangled herself and slipped to the ground at his side, making it easier for him to take note of his surroundings.

There wasn't very much to take note of. Just the wall and the bleak, desolate landscape. A few pebbles were scattered about, and—something small and globular and blubbery that was stirring in a cuplike hollow directly in front of Wayne.

Ruth cried out suddenly and plucked at his sleeve.

"Ken, look! That little egg thing is alive!"

An egg thing! Of course, it did resemble an egg. It was veined and oddly cracked and something wet was spilling out of it. Something projected from it too—the long shaft of an arrow.

Wayne's neck hairs rose. He got up and staggered toward the "egg," and as he did so, the whole surface of the wall swept into view. It bore an unmistakable resemblance to the Great Wall of China reduced to fairy-tale dimensions.

Rugged and battlemented it was, but small—not more than thirty feet in height at the tower sections and much lower in between. It curved in and out over the plain, under a sky of fiery blueness, to lose itself at the horizon's rim with a kind of down-sweeping rush that conveyed an illusion of motion.

The egg-shaped object had stopped moving when Wayne dropped to one knee beside it. The arrow had pierced it cruelly, and Wayne could not doubt that it had ceased to feel pain. The little white tadpole arms which sprouted from it were limp now, completely inert in the blue glare. Equally limp was its puckered, little-old-man face, the mouth hanging open, the heavily lidded eyes drained of all expression.

Wayne did not attempt to withdraw the arrow. Obviously the egg thing was dead. He was glad that it could not return his stare. He arose and turned to Ruth.

"It was alive!" he said. "A ghastly little animal with an almost human face, shaped like an egg. I can't believe—"

Twang!

As the arrow sped past Wayne, he leaped back with a startled cry. Something huge and blue had come out from behind a bend in the wall to aim a bow at him. He caught a brief, terrifying glimpse of it as it darted back into shadows.

Wayne turned abruptly and gripped his companion's arm. "We've got to get away from here as quickly as possible," he whispered with hoarse urgency.

"Away?" Ruth stared. "How can we? The machine has disappeared."

"We must get away from this wall. There's something deadly here that shoots to kill!"

"Human beings?"

"Man-shaped beings. Angular, flattish. They don't seem to have any heads."

Ruth swayed toward him. "Are you sure they're shooting at us?"

"We can't wait to find out. We've got to run for it."

"Where do you think we are?" Ruth breathed in sick horror. "Another dimension?"

Before Wayne could reply, another arrow sped past them with a vibrant twang.

They broke into a run, keeping close to the wall, their shadows preceding them in the blue glimmering. Panting, terrified, they came to a brief halt beneath a darkly looming tower that seemed to bulge out over the plain.

At right angles to the wall, a hundred feet from where they were standing, a vast circular mound bisected the plain, its edges misty in the strange light.

"Come on!" Wayne urged. "That mound may be hollow. We've got to chance it."

They were in motion again, racing toward the mound, when they heard a fluttering sound. It seemed to beat out from the mound in tangible waves, like the stirring of migratory birds gathering in great numbers in a tree and shaking the air with their flutterings.

Then up from the mound twenty or thirty winged black shapes soared, spiraling up into the sky in a wild, soaring ecstasy of flight. Almost instantly the arrows started flying.

One by one the birds dropped like dead sticks to the ground amidst a flurry of deadly arrows. With hoarse cawings they dropped, their feathers flying, their long, lizardlike bodies pierced by the cruel shafts.

Back into the mound they dropped, straight down with their flutterings stilled.

For a moment there was complete stillness on the plain, unearthly, terrifying.

Then Wayne said in a choked voice: "Does all this remind you of something? In a vague, distorted, nightmarish way, I mean? Does it?"

Ruth stared across the plain before replying. It seemed to her that she saw shadows, angular, menacing, moving in the distance, on the rim of her vision. It seemed to her that she saw the shadows of bows, blue on the plain. "Humpty Dumpty sat on a wall!" she said. "Six and twenty blackbirds—baked into a pie!"

"You thought of that too, did you?" Wayne's lips were white. "We didn't see Humpty Dumpty fall, but it was a great fall he had.

It smashed him, and not all the King's horses and all the King's men—"

"Stop it!" Ruth's voice was almost a scream. "There are no horses, no King's men here. That egg was a hideous little animal with the face of an ape. And blackbirds don't have lizardlike bodies."

A procession came around the mouth with a far-off beating of tiny drums. It could not be said that they were King's horses or King's men. They were something not quite rational.

It was a winding procession of egg-things, tottering on little stumpy legs, and prancing green shapes that bore a startling resemblance to walking-stick insects. The eggs were linked together by dangling wisps of filmy stuff. When they came closer, the filmy stuff resolved itself into a net, glimmering, metallic.

They're going to catch Humpty Dumpty when he falls, Wayne thought wildly.

Suddenly the long wall stirred with activity. A dozen little egg-shapes were running along it, dodging and weaving, their tadpole forelimbs quivering.

A shadow, dark, ominous, moved on the plain.

Twang!

The running eggs splintered as they fell. A wailing went up from the advancing procession, long-drawn, shrill. The "King's horses" swerved in closer to the wall, the net floating free.

Too late! The ground was littered with writhing and dying egg-shapes, shattered, spilling their yolks. One was not writhing. It was completely bashed in, a flattish horror swimming in its yolk.

Suddenly Ruth screamed, "Look over there! It's one of those angular, headless things. It's aiming at us!"

The blue bowman had stepped out from the shadow of the wall and was sharply limned in the downslanting radiance. His arms and legs were metallic zigzags, his body an angular shaft. He was slim-waisted, broad-shouldered, a Zeus lightning bolt aping the human form, a cut-out shape like a figure on a lampshade, standing poised and vibrant as he raised his bow.

Wayne swung about, took hold of Ruth, and dragged her to the ground. The arrow twanged horribly as it left the bow. They could feel death brushing them as the ghastly, headless figure sprang back into shadows.

Then they were in motion again. They headed straight for the mound, past the procession of toddling ovoids and prancing walking sticks, their faces livid with terror. Another arrow sped past them, raising a flurry of dust as it thudded into the base of the mound.

Then they were climbing up over a tumbled rampart of thrown-up earth and down into a hollow rimmed with blue shadows that seemed to leap toward them out of the gloom.

"That took courage," a quiet voice said.

The man was sitting on a boulder with a Seral hand blaster cradled in his arms. He was a big man, with massive shoulders and a gaunt-featured face. He had torn off his shirt and made a bandage of it. He sat blinking against the light, his right arm wrapped in the bandage, his eyes deep pools of torment. Empty cartridges lay scattered about his feet.

He smiled wryly and started to rise, then thought better of it.

"I'm James Bryce!" he said. "How did you get here?"

He gestured toward another boulder as he spoke. "Sit down, man. You're safe for the moment. I've been holding them off with carefully timed blasts."

Wayne helped Ruth to the boulder and stood for an instant with his back to Bryce, breathing heavily as he stared across the plain. Then he swung about. Words poured from him, a torrent of words.

When he had finished, Bryce nodded grimly. "I see! Pretty gruesome from start to finish. We're trapped in a world we never dreamed existed, and—we've the Orban boy to thank for it!"

Ruth spoke then. "*Mother Goose*," she whispered. "*The Old English Nursery Rhymes*. A world that exists only in the Orban boy's mind. Somehow he's made it real, three-dimensional."

Bryce smiled oddly. "You've been thinking that? It's not true, but it does you credit. It means you have at least a toe-hold on reality. You know that reality can't be reshaped to any kind of pre-conceived mental pattern."

Bryce forced a crooked smile. "What would another dimension be like, logically? Peopled with men and women like ourselves? A mathematician's pipe dream?

"Rubbish, don't you think? Why should intelligence in another world function on a plane that's comprehensible to us? Take the dreams that have found their way into the literature of childhood. What is the literature of childhood? Isn't it, in its purest essence, a world of nightmare fantasy and diffuse cruelty, without rhyme or reason?"

He looked up quickly. "Humpty Dumpty sat on a wall, Humpty Dumpty had a great fall. What made him fall? Poor old Humpty Dumpty! Weep for him—rush to the wall and watch the poor, pitiful attempts that will be made to put him together again.

"Nothing cruel about poor old Humpty Dumpty. He'd tear your heart out. A lovely, goofy old egg. Where's the cruelty then? I'll tell you. The picture that devilish fantasy conjures up is the essence of cruelty. A smashed, quivering, alive egg, in torment, scattered, spilling its yolk."

"But—"

Bryce waved a muscular hand. "The world of a child's reading is like a pack of tarot cards. You know the old stories of children bewitched and tormented by cruel goblins. There's a grotesquerie in it like nothing on earth.

"A child's mind is wide open to it—receptive. A child really sees into that world, in its dreams. Do you know why? That world really exists—as a sober scientific reality. When we grow up, we forget to remember."

Bryce's lips tightened. "A child's mental receptivity isn't blunted by the world around it. It grows up in two worlds at once, until it adjusts to our reality. But the author of the *Mother Goose* rhymes remembered his dreams of childhood more vividly than most men."

Bryce made a deprecatory gesture. "The real Humpty Dumpties are quite a bit different. Living ovoids who are always the victims of a cruel sport, destined to be shot down, and rescued too late by their little stricken fellows.

"There's a doom on all of them. What a weird, wild, shooting-gallery world this is! Sport, archery. The headless archers. They're cocks of the walk here, I think, swaggering, slim-waisted bullies. But there's something automatic about them. I don't think they're prime movers."

"I'm glad to know that," Wayne grunted grimly.

"The prime movers who created this world may be a kind of puppet master without visible substance. What impressed me from the instant I arrived here was the automatic, clockwork aspect of everything. It's intangible, hard to pin down. But a sensitive man can hardly fail to be aware of it."

"I know what you mean," Ruth whispered.

"Everything's cyclic. Those blackbirds ascend like clay pigeons released in swarms at intervals, and when the eggs fall, others take their places on the wall. We haven't penetrated very deeply into this world. Old Mother Hubbard may be here too, with a ravenous dog that isn't a dog, really.

"It may be a dog that keeps going to an empty hole in a cliff wall. He rushes in, barking furiously, and comes out without a bone. The cupboard is bare. Then an arrow pierces him, and he's a dead dog for a while. Jack and Jill go up a hill, a target for the headless archers.

"They're Jack and Jill in the nursery rhymes. Here they may be angular, metallic figures, but horribly vulnerable. The pail of water is shattered, spills, and runs like quicksilver into the ground. Jack and Jill pick themselves up, pluck out the arrows, and go staggering back up the hill to get some more water, their faces writhing in agony. Or maybe there are Jack-and-Jill replacements and the first pair die!"

Bryce's gaunt face was deadly pale now in the chill blue light. "It's a hellish clock set in motion and staying in motion," he added.

"The Orban boy knew what this world was like," Wayne said slowly. "He called the archers blue bowmen. How does he fit into it?"

"Remember his strange destiny!" Bryce answered. "That's the crux of it, man! He—"

Bryce stiffened in sudden wariness, tightening his grip on the blaster. "Here they come," he warned. "Keep your shoulders down. They converge, shooting with ugly deliberation. But blasting scatters them."

As he spoke, three blue archers came into view between the wall and the mound. They emerged from shadows to stand motionless for an instant on the plain.

Sweat ran cold on Wayne's back. The upraised bows were trained on the mound, taut and glittering arcs of metal bisected by gleaming arrowheads. The shanks of the arrows were drawn back by hands like mailed fists, the bowstrings beaded with light.

The archers released their bows simultaneously. There was a single sound, like the crack of a whiplash in utter stillness.

It was followed by a dull roar. Smoke swirled from the mound as Bryce blasted, blotting the archers from view. When it cleared, two of the original archers were lying prostrate, but their numbers had been augmented fivefold.

Bryce was cursing softly and holding on to his bandaged arm. "Caught an arrow when I came through," he muttered. "That concussion opened up the wound. Why did it have to be my right arm?"

"Here, let me take that!" Wayne said, wrenching at the blaster.

"I can handle it!" Bryce grunted in angry protest. But Wayne had the blaster now and was aiming it at the headless figures, his lips a bowstring line.

Twang!

One arrow, for an instant that seemed a lifetime, cleaving the air. Then came a dozen arrows, a hundred, in a swirl of brightness above Ruth's terror-wrenched face.

Wayne blasted not once, but four times in hot anger, his throat a throbbing ache. The energy flare blotted out the plain. A blinding pulsebeat seemed to throb in the heart of the blast amidst an expanding whiteness.

When the smoke thinned out, the plain was littered with recumbent archers. A few were shattered. It was incredibly nerve-torturing to watch metallic zigzags twitch and pick themselves up and whip away into shadows like seared leaves.

"That was reckless!" Bryce grunted. "A single blast would have stopped them just as effectively. They can't stand the shattering repercussions!"

Wayne sucked in his breath. For an instant he remained in a crouching attitude, his eyes bright with horror. Then he stood up. "I asked you how the Orban boy fitted into this," he said grimly. "Let's have the rest of it."

Bryce shrugged. "Consider, man. For generations kids have been brought up on a diet of fantasy and reality. One offsets the other. Children don't know how real the fantasy world is, and the reality around them quickly blots out Humpty Dumpty."

"Well?"

"The Orban boy knew how to read, and the fantasy world took on an unnatural brilliance for him. It became his own intimate, private world. He had just the stars of space to look at, and that inward vision. Don't you see? He had to get to it. He had to break through the dimensional barrier. It became an obsession with him."

"But how?"

"There were technical, scientific books on that ship. The Orban boy knew how to read, and he wasn't an animal. He was whiplash smart. Even at eight, he had a working grasp of applied physics. He'd talked a lot with his father, knew how to tinker."

Bryce kicked at a loose stone with his toe. "Perfectly normal boys of eight have had I.Q.'s of one-fifty. Mozart was an accomplished musician at six—a great one at nine. Boy chess wizards crop up in every generation, and chess is a three-way game. You've got to peg your naked intelligence into a background of semantics and applied psychology. But some kids get monumental backgrounds just by keeping their eyes and ears open.

"What do we know about human intelligence anyway? Illiterate rustics have mastered atomic theory using hit-and-miss techniques. The Orban boy was precocious, granted. But we know even less about precocity than we do about adult intelligence."

Bryce looked at Wayne with a torturing surmise. "That kid slipped away from us for a couple of hours, got to his father's workshop. Sheer carelessness on our part. When I saw him with the machine, I rushed out of the house and tried to reason with him. We got into an argument, and I started tugging at him.

"Luckily I'd strapped a Seral blaster to my hip, just in case. But it was the blaster that got in my way. It weighed me down—in the wrong direction. When I tripped, I didn't have a chance of regaining my balance."

Bryce shrugged grimly. "I've been holding the archers at bay ever since. Funny thing about that machine. It's light—weighs about eight pounds. Orban can carry it, but if you stand directly in front of it, your goose is cooked. After I came through, I didn't see the machine. It must be invisible from this side!"

Wayne nodded. "We didn't see it either!"

"It's still around, I imagine. When I came through, an archer saw me. I caught an arrow in my shoulder. I ripped it out and hurled it from me, and it vanished in a flash of light. You say you saw an arrow come out. Probably it was the same arrow."

Wayne started to speak, but Bryce stopped him. "Listen!" he warned.

From the purple-hollowed middle of the mound there arose a

strange, mournful, dirgelike sound. Then up from the mound came a dozen "blackbirds," their lizardlike bodies quivering as they went spiraling into the sky.

No arrows pursued them. There was utter silence on the plain.

"Looks as though we've thrown a scare into the archers for the time being," Wayne muttered, but there was no exaltation in his voice.

Bryce shook his head. "They'll attack again," he said with grim conviction. "Those birds were simply lucky this time. I wonder if they realize how lucky—or care!"

Ruth whispered: "Six and twenty blackbirds, baked into a pie! When the pie was opened, the birds began to sing! My, what a dainty dish to set before a king!"

Her voice rose sharply. "Ken, who do you suppose the king was? We haven't seen him! Is there a king?"

"A symbolic embellishment," Bryce snapped. "I'll say it again: *Mother Goose* is simply this world seen through the distorted mirror of a child's imagination. The author of *Mother Goose* transformed what he saw here into a medieval fairy tale. We'll never see the king because we have nothing in common with him."

The sky seemed to darken as Bryce spoke. Wayne looked up in chill apprehension, a shudder coursing up his spine.

"Oh, no!" Ruth choked.

But there *was* something high in the sky, swinging slowly down toward the mound. Something globular that wore what looked like a shining crown and shook like a mound of jelly.

Nearer it came and nearer, swinging lower with each vibration of its circular bulk.

It blazed suddenly into sharp visibility. It wasn't a king, and it wore no crown. It was a floating spheroid, veined and translucent, filled with an intricate assortment of moving parts that gave off a continuous whirring sound.

A madness seemed to possess Wayne as he stared up at it. He cupped his hands and shouted: "Who are you?"

"Who are you?" came back in a staccato echo.

"Who are you?"

"Who are you?"

"If it says: 'Who am I?' I'll die!" Ruth screamed hysterically.

"Who am I?" the spheroid flung out. "I'll die!"

"Wait!" Bryce gripped Ruth's arm, his lips shaking. "It's a tropism—nothing more. A kind of echo response. You soft-pedaled the 'If it says'—then screamed the rest. It only picked up the last part. It didn't change the question. It simply repeats what it picks up!"

"No—it doesn't," Ruth groaned. "Now it's going to say: 'You'll die!'"

"Not unless you scream it first," Bryce said with a brittle laugh. "Look, I'll show you."

He cupped his hands. "You're going to win through," he shouted.

"You're going to win through!" came back.

"It's a promise," Bryce shouted.

"It's a promise!"

"You see?" Bryce turned with a relieved grimace. "You seldom get a better answer than that. It's a regular politician's answer. What you want to hear comes back in vibrant echo that means absolutely nothing."

The gear-and-wheel-filled spheroid was swinging back now, straight up into the sky. It dwindled rapidly, vibrating as it swept from view.

"Well, that was your 'king,'" Bryce said. "I've a hunch it's simply a weird regulatory mechanism that sweeps down at long intervals. A kind of cog in the clockwork setup—a stabilizing flying pendulum that's needed here to keep things moving on an even keel."

Ruth sprang back with a gasp of horror. Three tiny metallic shapes had scurried swiftly over the edge of the hollow and were descending into the blackbird pit with the blindly groping movements of terrified moles.

Moles? Why not mice? Blind mice?

Wayne was the first to say it. "Three blind mice, see how they run—" He stopped, appalled.

"Finish it," Bryce muttered. "They all ran up to the farmer's wife, who cut off their tails with a carving knife."

He gestured eloquently. "I told you cruelty was of the essence here. It's a savage, senseless, last-turn-of-the-screw kind of cruelty. Why mutilate blind mice? Isn't that utterly ghastly? And yet it's in *Mother Goose*.

"There's hardly a *Mother Goose* rhyme that doesn't shadow forth this world. The hunters and—the hunted. Creatures pursued by blind cruelty, shot down in flight. Who killed Cock Robin?"

A grim puzzlement seemed to grip Bryce. "Cock Robin! That's the cruelest one of all. It's so devilish in its wicked, eerie malice that some editors of *Mother Goose* omit it entirely, as not for children!"

He frowned. "Just who was Cock Robin anyway? Why was everyone so horrified? Cock Robin with his bleeding breast, the taut and quivering arrow. Why was Cock Robin so different, almost a stranger to this world? Why did the cruelty pause to wonder? Why did everyone answer: 'Not I! Not I!'

"Why did everyone single out Cock Robin as the one creature in this world who shouldn't have been killed at all?"

Bryce strode back and forth, glancing over the mound as if in chill apprehension.

"A curious thing! Not only the *Mother Goose* rhymes shadow forth this world. An ancient Chinese vase bears the inscription: 'See how the harsh blackbirds fly into the bronze sun, pursued by the arrows of darkness!'

"And Lewis Carroll! There are things in *Alice in Wonderland* that seem to shadow forth this world. Why was *Alice* so real to generations of children?"

He shrugged. "A few men remembered their childhood visions well, apparently. Too well for comfort. The looking glass was simply a symbol. You step through. The Orban boy got at the scientific reality behind the symbol. He actually constructed a dimension-dissolving looking glass!"

Ruth stared at him. "Are you claiming that all children are dangerous little monsters?"

Bryce shook his head. "No. Only very special children. Children who were cut off from all normal activity, as Orban was. Their visions spur them on. But I think we've always known, subconsciously, that a child with too much knowledge would be dangerous. Why do people like to make up rhymes about the wickedness of children? Remember the Little Willie rhymes:

> *"Little Willie hung his sister*
> *She was dead before we missed her!*

Willie's always up to tricks!
Ain't he cute? He's only six."

From somewhere on the plain came an answering whisper, as though the cruel words had goaded the blue world to activity again. A low rustling swept across the plain, ominous, mind-chilling.

"Here they come!" Bryce whispered, reaching for the blaster.

Wayne moved quickly to forestall him. He had the weapon and was leveling it before the psychologist could glower in protest.

A shadow fell on the plain, grew larger. The blue archers were stepping out from the wall with a deadly deliberation, their Zeus-taut bodies wrapped in a translucent glimmering.

Wayne held his fire until a dozen archers released their bows simultaneously. There was a pulsing at his temples as the trigger clicked. A swirl of whiteness followed the click, a silent whiteness for an instant as brief as a dropped heartbeat. Then a thunderous concussion shook the mound, hurling him backward....

AN HOUR later, Wayne sat with his back to the tumbled earth rampart, his face haggard with strain. A thin smoke was swirling over the mound, an acrid haze which obscured the slope directly below him and blotted out the crouching bulk of Bryce. But he could feel the despair which emanated from Bryce—a palpable force. Bryce spoke suddenly. "I'm glad we saved one blast!" he muttered. "We've got to decide how to use it!"

The words fell on a chill, deadly silence.

Then Ruth uttered a sobbing moan. Wayne knew with grim certainty that Bryce would not attempt to spare her. If he thought the blaster should be turned upon the hollow and held in steady hands, he would say so.

They sat silently together for an instant, not daring to voice what was in their minds.

Then Bryce spoke directly to Ruth. "By heaven, you're a pretty woman!"

A sudden, hot anger swept over Wayne like a flood of molten lava.

"If we had any chance at all," Bryce added, heavily, "Ken would have a rival!"

Wayne suddenly realized that Bryce had more delicacy than he had given him credit for. He had chosen an odd way to announce that there was no hope, but Wayne was glad that he had not phrased it brutally. His anger evaporated.

Twang!

The arrow sped in close, barely missing Wayne. The archers were in motion again. As they drew in toward the mound, their bows thrumming, the air grew thick with deadly arrows in flight.

There was a continuous deadly twanging, a drumming in the air, a drumming in Wayne's skull—a reeling giddiness. Wayne did not hesitate or swing about to voice an agonized doubt. The suddenness of the attack had settled the issue for him.

The last blast would not be guided by another man's caution. His decision was made, and nothing could alter it.

Wayne blasted with a quick intake of his breath.

The spurting radiation struck the plain with a mighty roar. Wayne felt again the shattering recoil, the shoulder-bruising impact of a heavy weapon leaping in his clasp.

For an instant fire and smoke danced on the plain, swirling over the base of the mound and blotting the archers from view.

Then the smoke thinned and rolled back over a seared expanse of desolation the more awful because it wasn't quite empty. One archer was still advancing, swaying a little as it climbed the slope through the dissolving smoke, its bow upraised.

The archer was almost at the crest of the mound when Wayne sprung straight at it. With a sickening twang, the arrow left the bow and thudded into the earth rampart at Wayne's back. Then Wayne was beating with the blaster against the archer's angular body, swinging with it again and again, pounding with all his strength.

The plain rang with the harsh, strident clang of metal against metal, as though knights in a tourney were colliding head on in a suicidal contest of strength.

With a savageness that amazed him, Wayne fought the archer back down the slope. Eyes wild, lips quivering, he brought the sharp edge of his weapon against the horror's gleaming chest and slashed downward at the low-slung metal quiver at its waist.

Strange how much courage a man had when his life was forfeit, strange the shining strength, like a shield around the heart, blazing out for all to see!

Arrows were spilling from the archer's quiver and its body was twisting strangely when something seemed to lift it up and hurl it backward toward the wall. Wayne cried out hoarsely as the writhing horror receded from him, twisting and turning like a gale-lashed leaf. It vanished abruptly, in a blinding flash of light.

And as it vanished, a running figure came into view on the plain.

"Orban!"

It was Ruth who shouted it, coming to her feet in wild disbelief. The Orban boy was running straight toward Wayne and waving his arms in urgent appeal.

Wayne couldn't catch what the Orban boy was shouting. But he could see that the running lad was gesturing him back toward the mound.

In a daze of fevered uncertainty, Wayne swung about and started climbing. He heard himself sobbing. His legs threatened to give out, but he managed to gain the crest and fling himself down in the hollow. He lay on his stomach, staring over the rampart, his lungs choked with dust.

Slowly he became aware that Ruth had thrown herself down beside him and was clinging to him in sobbing relief.

The Orban boy came over the crest with his breath coming in choking gasps. He flung himself down directly opposite Wayne and raised himself on one elbow.

"Had to wait—until I was sure I could get you out," he breathed. "That man—" He gestured toward Bryce. "He's not so important, but you're my friend! Had to save you, Ken!"

Wayne stared, his mouth strangely dry.

"My idea was to hide the machine until I was equipped to come into this world, Ken." Orban went on feverishly. "I worked something out, but it wasn't good enough to protect me in here. That's why I asked you to help me hide the machine!"

"Just what did you work out?" Bryce asked. His face was ashen, but his voice was firm enough.

"Just met Ken last night," the Orban boy wheezed, his eyes shining. "But he's the only friend I ever had. He was going to hide me. That's more than you'd do, I bet."

"You're right about that," Bryce said with a harsh laugh. "I asked you, What did you work out?"

For reply, the Orban boy opened his hand. The object which

rested on his palm was small, no larger than a jackknife. It was shaped like a compass. Six tiny glowing knobs projected from it, but otherwise it was unbelievably makeshift in aspect, as though the Orban boy had walked into a toyshop, picked up a compass, and twisted two wires intricately around the floating needle. And now he was displaying his prize with a fierce pride, as though he'd done something remarkable.

"Worked hard at it, in Ken's kitchen," the Orban boy explained. "Took me six hours to get it right."

"You're sure it works now?"

"You bet I'm sure," Orban said pridefully. "The segments which feed that loop have been moved around, see? They pass right under the contact points. All I have to do is draw the second loop into position by the attraction of the needle."

As he spoke, the Orban boy pressed one of the little knobs on the rim of the "compass." The "compass" lighted up.

"Now it's ready!" Orban said.

Bryce stared. "Ready for what?"

The Orban boy cupped his palm over the "compass."

"You'll see. Watch!"

Light from the "compass" streamed out between the Orban boy's fingers and haloed his entire hand. Slowly he raised his hand and turned to Wayne with a triumphant cry.

"Look at what is happening!"

It was impossible not to look. The blue world was in sudden, furious activity. Down from the sky the "King" wobbled, to hang directly over the mound. The blind mice ran backward out of the blackbird pit, and six and twenty blackbirds rose into the sky. And out on the plain stepped a dozen blue archers, their bows upraised.

But the most terrifying thing was the gulf which yawned suddenly on the plain. Out of it stumbled something that looked like a jigsaw giant, bent nearly double. The figure went reeling and stumbling over the plain as if in unendurable agony.

The figure was metallic, very similar to the archers, but it moved in a dizzying crooked way that brought a tortured reeling to Wayne's mind.

"'There was a crooked man, and he ran a crooked mile,'" Ruth heard herself screaming.

Twang!

An arrow pierced the blueness, thudding into the shoulders of the crazily weaving figure. The giant stumbled and fell forward, its loose-jointed arms flailing the air. It dragged itself crookedly backward toward the trapdoor in the plain, its movements still geometrically insane.

Suddenly the archers froze. They stood rigid, unmoving, their bows held at grotesque angles. The "King" stopped vibrating. It hung motionless above the mound, congealed into the blueness like an ice-frozen jellyfish.

Every other object within view took on an aspect of rigidity. All movement ceased. There was a stillness so absolute, even the stirring of a blind mouse would have set up a din. But the mice were stiff, rigid, impaled in a web of stillness.

"By heaven, he's stopped the clock!"

Bryce's stunned cry shattered the human stillness on the mound. But the "King" did not echo back the sound, and nothing on the plain moved.

Orban grinned then, for the first time. "I knew it would work," he exulted. "It had to work. It'll all start up again, in just about three minutes. Can't stop it for long. You've got to get out fast."

"You mean," Bryce wet his shaking lips. "That little thing"— he waved one arm—"stopped *all that?*"

"Size hasn't a thing to do with power," the Orban boy said, as though he were addressing a child. "Shucks, I could blow up every city on earth—big cities like New York and Chicago—with something half the size of this!"

Ruth swayed.

"I fixed the machine so you can see it from this side," Orban said. "When you go out, I'll break it up from this side. Come on, Ken. You got to get around that wall before it all starts up again."

All four of them started off in the direction Orban indicated, running at top speed.

Nerve-torturing thoughts that fitted no pattern of sanity or logic were churning about at the back of Wayne's mind as he dashed after the youth. They rounded the wall in a run, the Orban boy in the lead, Bryce bringing up the rear.

The wall hadn't changed, but the toppled Humpty Dumpties resembled eggs that had dropped from a cold-storage crate. Their tadpole arms had ceased to jerk, and their spilled yolks were frozen solid.

The Orban boy paused an instant to nudge an egg with his toe. "The poor little thing!" he murmured, shaking his head. Then he was in motion again.

When the machine swept into view, the Orban boy was breathing heavily, his face tight with strain. But he kept on running until he was directly in front of it. Then he turned and waited for the others to come up.

"I can't go with you, Ken," he said when Wayne reached his side. "I belong here. Always have—always will!"

He shuffled his feet as he spoke, and suddenly he was thrusting out his hand.

Wayne stared at him in stunned horror. "But you can't remain!" he protested. "When those devilish archers start up again—"

Orban shook his head, squinting back at the wall. "I don't dare leave, Ken! Know what would happen if I did? I'd get careless, and there'd be more accidents. People would get killed—everybody on earth, maybe. I know so much in some ways—I'm not safe to be trusted!"

The Orban boy was behind the machine, and he was rushing straight toward Ken with the machine held out before him.

It was a little like passing into a warm shower. The light was all around Wayne, lashing against him, before he realized that he was no longer on the plain.

"Good-bye, Ken!" came in a dwindling echo of sound. "Sure was great to have a friend!"

Wayne picked himself up from the floor and looked around him. He wasn't alone in the room. Ruth was sitting beside him. Bryce lay on the floor, and the croquet wicket was dwindling to a shapeless lump of metal in a dwindling blaze of light.

Bryce was getting slowly to his feet and staring about him with fiercely contracted brows as though he despised Wayne's taste in furnishings and was about to say so.

Bryce went to a chair and sat down. "Nice place you have here, Ken," he said.

Suddenly his composure broke. Sweat came out on his face, the back of his hands. He shuddered.

"He'll never come back," he whispered. "We've seen the last of him."

Wayne got up and staggered back against the wall and stared at Bryce.

Bryce made a despairing gesture. "I wish now I'd said a few kind words to him. It was the least I could have done."

"Why?" Wayne was hardly aware that he had spoken.

"Oh, it's a paradox, all right," Bryce murmured. "Just like— the paradox of time travel. Say a man lives now and goes into the past. Doesn't that mean he's always existed in the past? But how can he go back to where he's always been?"

Ruth had gotten up and was staring at Bryce with startled eyes. "What has that to do with the Orban boy?" she asked.

"Say you went into another dimension today," Bryce said slowly. "Say it was a kind of timeless dimension—from our point of view. Wouldn't you in a sense exist in that other world from the very creation of that world? Wouldn't you freeze into that world and become a part of it from the start?"

"If someone from our world saw that other world centuries ago, wouldn't he find you there? I think he would."

Bryce paused an instant to stare out the window of Wayne's living room. The murk of an October morning stretched beyond the pane. He stared at Wayne, then at Ruth, as though challenging them to deny that they had just returned from a quite different world.

"You saw that King-clock horror swinging down from the sky!" he went on. "A mechanical tropism enabled it to echo back sound. Suppose a boy, who never should have gone into that world, was trapped in it. Suppose he shouted his defiance to the sky as the arrows sped toward him.

"Suppose he shouted his name, in anger and fierce pride, recklessly, as a defiant boy might well be tempted to do. His name, now and forever, long before he was born into our world, our time, because he'd made himself a timeless part of that timeless world."

"Well?" Wayne's voice was a puzzled whisper.

"A good many boys have nicknames. Young Orban's given name was Phillip, but his father didn't call him that."

Ruth gave a cry. "No! Oh, no!"

"Suppose the King-clock merely repeated the name," Bryce said gently. "Suppose the boy lay slain on the plain, and the King repeated his name, over and over. And the little lad who was to write *Mother Goose* saw that world in a dream of childhood and heard the name. The author of *Mother Goose* must have been an imaginative child.

"Remember—he saw the horror only dimly. It bore the name of a familiar bird. Why not a bird lying slain on the plain and everyone in that world asking: 'Who killed Cock Robin? Not I? Not I?' Everyone horrified, appalled, because Cock Robin was a stranger in that world."

"You mean—"

"It was an intangible thing, the uniqueness of Cock Robin, but it must have communicated itself to the author of *Mother Goose*. He imagined the rest, the protesting voices, the shared horror and remorse. He made a fantastic little nursery rhyme about it."

Bryce looked at Ruth. "Do you know who Cock Robin was now?" he asked.

Ruth drew closer to Wayne before she spoke, as though she dared not remain alone with such a burden of horror and pity resting its cold weight on her heart.

"His father called him Robin!" she whispered. "Robin! Robin! The Orban boy—he was Cock Robin!"

THE SKY TRAP

Lawton enjoyed a good fight. He stood happ[y]
with Slashaway Tommy, his lean-fleshed torso gleam.... ᵧ
sweat. He preferred to work the pugnacity out of himself slowly, to
savor it as it ebbed.

"Better luck next time, Slashaway," he said, and unlimbered a
left hook that thudded against his opponent's jaw with such violence that the big, hairy ape crumpled to the resin and rolled over
on his back.

Lawton brushed a lock of rust-colored hair back from his
brow and stared down at the limp figure lying on the descending
stratoship's slightly tilted athletic deck.

"Good work, Slashaway," he said. "You're primitive and
beetle-browed, but you've got what it takes."

Lawton flattered himself that he was the opposite of primitive.
High in the sky he had predicted the weather for eight days running, with far more accuracy than he could have put into a punch.

They'd flash his report all over Earth in a couple of minutes
now. From New York to London to Singapore and back. In half an
hour he'd be donning street clothes and stepping out feeling
darned good.

He had fulfilled his weekly obligation to society by manipu-
lating meteorological instruments for forty-five minutes, high in
the warm, upper stratosphere and worked off his pugnacity by
knocking down a professional gym slugger. He would have a full,
glorious week now to work off all his other drives.

The stratoship's commander, Captain Forrester, had come
up, and was staring at him reproachfully. "Dave, I don't hold with
the reforming Johnnies who want to re-make human nature from
the ground up. But you've got to admit our generation knows how
to keep things humming with a minimum of stress. We don't have
world wars now because we work off our pugnacity by sailing into
gym sluggers eight or ten times a week. And since our romantic
emotions can be taken care of by tactile television we're not at the
mercy of every brainless bit of fluff's calculated ankle appeal."

Lawton turned, and regarded him quizzically. "Don't you
suppose I realize that? You'd think I just blew in from Mars."

"All right. We have the outlets, the safety valves. They are sup-
posed to keep us civilized. But you don't derive any benefit from
them."

"The heck I don't. I exchange blows with Slashaway every
time I board the Perseus. And as for women—well, there's just one
woman in the world for me, and I wouldn't exchange her for all
the Turkish images in the tactile broadcasts from Stamboul."

"Yes, I know. But you work off your primitive emotions with
too much gusto. Even a cast-iron gym slugger can bruise. That last
blow was—brutal. Just because Slashaway gets thumped and
thudded all over by the medical staff twice a week doesn't mean he
can take—"

The stratoship lurched suddenly. The deck heaved up under
Lawton's feet, hurling him against Captain Forrester and spinning both men around so that they seemed to be waltzing together
across the ship. The still limp gym slugger slid downward, colliding with a corrugated metal bulkhead and sloshing back and
forth like a wet mackerel.

A full minute passed before Lawton could put a stop to that.
Even while careening he had been alive to Slashaway's peril, and
had tried to leap to his aid. But the ship's steadily increasing gyrations had hurled him away from the skipper and against a massive
vaulting horse, barking the flesh from his shins and spilling him
with violence onto the deck.

He crawled now toward the prone gym slugger on his hands
and knees, his temples thudding. The gyrations ceased an instant
before he reached Slashaway's side. With an effort he lifted the big
man up, propped him against the bulkhead and shook him until
his teeth rattled. "Slashaway," he muttered. "Slashaway, old
fellow."

Slashaway opened blurred eyes, "Phew!" he muttered. "You
sure socked me hard, sir."

"You went out like a light," explained Lawton gently. "A
minute before the ship lurched."

"The ship *lurched*, sir?"

"Something's very wrong, Slashaway. The ship isn't moving.
There are no vibrations and—Slashaway, are you hurt? Your skull
thumped against that bulkhead so hard I was afraid—"

"Naw, I'm okay. Whatd'ya mean, the ship ain't moving? How
could it stop?"

Lawton said. "I don't know, Slashaway." Helping the gym slugger to his feet he stared apprehensively about him. Captain Forrester was kneeling on the resin testing his hocks for sprains with splayed fingers, his features twitching.

"Hurt badly, sir?"

The Commander shook his head. "I don't think so. Dave, we are twenty thousand feet up, so how in hell could we be stationary in space?"

"It's all yours, skipper."

"I must say you're helpful."

Forrester got painfully to his feet and limped toward the athletic compartment's single quartz port—a small circle of radiance on a level with his eyes. As the port sloped downward at an angle of nearly sixty degrees all he could see was a diffuse glimmer until he wedged his brow in the observation visor and stared downward.

Lawton heard him suck in his breath sharply. "Well, sir?"

"There are thin cirrus clouds directly beneath us. They're not moving."

Lawton gasped, the sense of being in an impossible situation swelling to nightmare proportions within him. What could have happened?

Directly behind him, close to a bulkhead chronometer, which was clicking out the seconds with unabashed regularity, was a misty blue visiplate that merely had to be switched on to bring the pilots into view.

The Commander hobbled toward it, and manipulated a rheostat. The two pilots appeared side by side on the screen, sitting amidst a spidery network of dully gleaming pipe lines and nichrome humidification units. They had unbuttoned their high-altitude coats and their stratosphere helmets were resting on their knees. The Jablochoff candle light which flooded the pilot room accentuated the haggardness of their features, which were a sickly cadaverous hue.

The captain spoke directly into the visiplate. "What's wrong with the ship?" he demanded. "Why aren't we descending? Dawson, you do the talking!"

One of the pilots leaned tensely forward, his shoulders jerking. "We don't know, sir. The rotaries went dead when the ship started gyrating. We can't work the emergency torps and the temperature is rising."

"But—it defies all logic," Forrester muttered. "How could a metal ship weighing tons be suspended in the air like a balloon? It is stationary, but it is not buoyant. We seem in all respects to be *frozen in*."

"The explanation may be simpler than you dream," Lawton said. "When we've found the key."

The Captain swung toward him. "Could *you* find the key, Dave?"

"I should like to try. It may be hidden somewhere on the ship, and then again, it may not be. But I should like to go over the ship with a fine-tooth comb, and then I should like to go over *outside*, thoroughly. Suppose you make me an emergency mate and give me a carte blanche, sir."

Lawton got his carte blanche. For two hours he did nothing spectacular, but he went over every inch of the ship. He also lined up the crew and pumped them. The men were as completely in the dark as the pilots and the now completely recovered Slashaway, who was following Lawton about like a doting seal.

"You're a right guy, sir. Another two or three cracks and my noggin would've split wide open."

"But not like an eggshell, Slashaway. Pig iron develops fissures under terrific pounding but your cranium seems to be more like tempered steel. Slashaway, you won't understand this, but I've got to talk to somebody and the Captain is too busy to listen.

"I went over the entire ship because I thought there might be a hidden source of buoyancy somewhere. It would take a lot of air bubbles to turn this ship into a balloon, but there are large vacuum chambers under the multiple series condensers in the engine room which conceivably could have sucked in a helium leakage from the carbon pile valves. And there are bulkhead porosities which could have clogged."

"Yeah," muttered Slashaway, scratching his head. "I see what you mean, sir."

"It was no soap. There's nothing *inside* the ship that could possibly keep us up. Therefore there must be something outside that isn't air. We know there *is* air outside. We've stuck our heads out and sniffed it. And we've found out a curious thing.

"Along with the oxygen there is water vapor, but it isn't H_2O.

It's HO. A molecular arrangement like that occurs in the upper Solar atmosphere, but nowhere on Earth. And there's a thin sprinkling of hydrocarbon molecules out there too. Hydrocarbon appears ordinarily as methane gas, but out there it rings up as CH. Methane is CH4. And there are also scandium oxide molecules making unfamiliar faces at us. And oxide of boron—with an equational limp."

"Gee," muttered Slashaway. "We're up against it, eh?"

Lawton was squatting on his hams beside an emergency 'chute opening on the deck of the Penguin's weather observatory. He was letting down a spliced beryllium plumb line, his gaze riveted on the slowly turning horizontal drum of a windlass which contained more than two hundred feet of gleaming metal cordage.

Suddenly as he stared the drum stopped revolving. Lawton stiffened, a startled expression coming into his face. He had been playing a hunch that had seemed as insane, rationally considered, as his wild idea about the bulkhead porosities. For a moment he was stunned, unable to believe that he had struck pay dirt. The winch indicator stood at one hundred and three feet, giving him a rich, fruity yield of startlement.

One hundred feet below him the plummet rested on something solid that sustained it in space. Scarcely breathing, Lawton leaned over the windlass and stared downward. There was nothing visible between the ship and the fleecy clouds far below except a tiny black dot resting on vacancy and a thin beryllium plumb line ascending like an interrogation point from the dot to the 'chute opening.

"You see something down there?" Slashaway asked.

Lawton moved back from the windlass, his brain whirling. "Slashaway there's a solid surface directly beneath us, but it's completely invisible."

"You mean it's like a frozen cloud, sir?"

"No, Slashaway. It doesn't shimmer, or deflect light. Congealed water vapor would sink instantly to earth."

"You think it's all around us, sir?"

Lawton stared at Slashaway aghast. In his crude fumblings the gym slugger had ripped a hidden fear right out of his subconsciousness into the light.

"I don't know, Slashaway," he muttered. "I'll get at that next."

A half hour later Lawton sat beside the captain's desk in the control room, his face drained of all color. He kept his gaze averted as he talked. A man who succeeds too well with an unpleasant task may develop a subconscious sense of guilt.

"Sir, we're suspended inside a hollow sphere which resembles a huge, floating soap bubble. Before we ripped through it it must have had a plastic surface. But now the tear has apparently healed over, and the shell all around us is as resistant as steel. We're completely bottled up, sir. I shot rocket leads in all directions to make certain."

The expression on Forrester's face sold mere amazement down the river. He could not have looked more startled if the nearer planets had yielded their secrets chillingly, and a super-race had appeared suddenly on Earth.

"Good God, Dave. Do you suppose something has happened to space?"

Lawton raised his eyes with a shudder. "Not necessarily, sir. Something has happened to *us*. We're floating through the sky in a huge, invisible bubble of some sort, but we don't know whether it has anything to do with space. It may be a meteorological phenomenon."

"You say we're floating?"

"We're floating slowly westward. The clouds beneath us have been receding for fifteen or twenty minutes now."

"Phew!" muttered Forrester. "That means we've got to—"

He broke off abruptly. The Perseus' radio operator was standing in the doorway, distress and indecision in his gaze. "Our reception is extremely sporadic, sir," he announced. "We can pick up a few of the stronger broadcasts, but our emergency signals haven't been answered."

"Keep trying," Forrester ordered.

"Aye, aye, sir."

The captain turned to Lawton. "Suppose we call it a bubble. Why are we suspended like this, immovably? Your rocket leads shot up, and the plumb line dropped one hundred feet. Why should the ship itself remain stationary?"

Lawton said: "The bubble must possess sufficient internal equilibrium to keep a big, heavy body suspended at its core. In other words, we must be suspended at the hub of converging energy lines."

"You mean we're surrounded by an electromagnetic field?"

Lawton frowned. "Not necessarily, sir. I'm simply pointing out that there must be an energy tug of *some* sort involved. Otherwise the ship would be resting on the inner surface of the bubble."

Forrester nodded grimly. "We should be thankful, I suppose, that we can move about inside the ship. Dave, do you think a man could descend to the inner surface?"

"I've no doubt that a man could, sir. Shall I let myself down?"

"Absolutely not. Damn it, Dave, I need your energies inside the ship. I could wish for a less impulsive first officer, but a man in my predicament can't be choosy."

"Then what *are* your orders, sir?"

"Orders? Do I have to order you to think? Is working something out for yourself such a strain? We're drifting straight toward the Atlantic Ocean. What do you propose to do about that?"

"I expect I'll have to do my best, sir."

Lawton's "best" conflicted dynamically with the captain's orders. Ten minutes later he was descending, hand over hand, on a swaying emergency ladder.

"Tough-fibered Davie goes down to look around," he grumbled.

He was conscious that he was flirting with danger. The air outside was breathable, but would the diffuse, unorthodox gases injure his lungs? He didn't know, couldn't be sure. But he had to admit that he felt all right *so far*. He was seventy feet below the ship and not at all dizzy. When he looked down he could see the purple domed summits of mountains between gaps in the fleecy cloud blanket.

He couldn't see the Atlantic Ocean—yet. He descended the last thirty feet with mounting confidence. At the end of the ladder he braced himself and let go.

He fell about six feet, landing on his rump on a spongy surface that bounced him back and forth. He was vaguely incredulous when he found himself sitting in the sky staring through his spread legs at clouds and mountains.

He took a deep breath. It struck him that the sensation of falling could be present without movement downward through space. He was beginning to experience such a sensation. His stomach twisted and his brain spun.

He was suddenly sorry he had tried this. It was so damnably

unnerving he was afraid of losing all emotional control. He stared up, his eyes squinting against the sun. Far above him the gleaming, wedge-shaped bulk of the Perseus loomed colossally, blocking out a fifth of the sky.

Lowering his right hand he ran his fingers over the invisible surface beneath him. The surface felt rubbery, moist.

He got swayingly to his feet and made a perilous attempt to walk through the sky. Beneath his feet the mysterious surface crackled, and little sparks flew up about his legs. Abruptly he sat down again, his face ashen.

From the emergency 'chute opening far above a massive head appeared. "You all right, sir," Slashaway called, his voice vibrant with concern.

"Well, I—"

"You'd better come right up, sir. Captain's orders."

"All right," Lawton shouted. "Let the ladder down another ten feet."

Lawton ascended rapidly, resentment smouldering within him. What right had the skipper to interfere? He had passed the buck, hadn't he?

Lawton got another bad jolt the instant he emerged through the 'chute opening. Captain Forrester was leaning against a parachute rack gasping for breath, his face a livid hue.

Slashaway looked equally bad. His jaw muscles were twitching and he was tugging at the collar of his gym suit.

Forrester gasped: "Dave, I tried to move the ship. I didn't know you were outside."

"Good God, you didn't know—"

"The rotaries backfired and used up all the oxygen in the engine room. Worse, there's been a carbonic oxide seepage. The air is contaminated throughout the ship. We'll have to open the ventilation valves immediately. I've been waiting to see if—if you could breathe down there. You're all right, aren't you? The air *is* breathable?"

Lawton's face was dark with fury. "I was an experimental rat in the sky, eh?"

"Look, Dave, we're all in danger. Don't stand there glaring at me. Naturally I waited. I have my crew to think of."

"Well, think of them. Get those valves open before we all have convulsions."

A half hour later charcoal gas was mingling with oxygen outside the ship, and the crew was breathing it in again gratefully. Thinly dispersed, and mixed with oxygen it seemed all right. But Lawton had misgivings. No matter how attenuated a lethal gas is it is never entirely harmless. To make matters worse, they were over the Atlantic Ocean.

Far beneath them was an emerald turbulence, half obscured by eastward moving cloud masses. The bubble was holding, but the morale of the crew was beginning to sag.

Lawton paced the control room. Deep within him unsuspected energies surged. "We'll last until the oxygen is breathed up," he exclaimed. "We'll have four or five days, at most. But we seem to be traveling faster than an ocean liner. With luck, we'll be in Europe before we become carbon dioxide breathers."

"Will that help matters, Dave?" said the captain wearily.

"If we can blast our way out, it will."

The Captain's sagging body jackknifed erect. "Blast our way out? What do you mean, Dave?"

"I've clamped expulsor disks on the cosmic ray absorbers and trained them downward. A thin stream of accidental neutrons directed against the bottom of the bubble may disrupt its energies—wear it thin. It's a long gamble, but worth taking. We're staking nothing, remember?"

Forrester sputtered: "Nothing but our lives! If you blast a hole in the bubble you'll destroy its energy balance. Did that occur to you? Inside a lopsided bubble we may careen dangerously or fall into the sea before we can get the rotaries started."

"I thought of that. The pilots are standing by to start the rotaries the instant we lurch. If we succeed in making a rent in the bubble we'll break out the helicoptic vanes and descend vertically. The rotaries won't backfire again. I've had their burnt-out cylinder heads replaced."

An agitated voice came from the visiplate on the captain's desk: "Tuning in, sir."

Lawton stopped pacing abruptly. He swung about and grasped the desk edge with both hands, his head touching Forrester's as the two men stared down at the horizontal face of petty officer James Caldwell.

Caldwell wasn't more than twenty-two or three, but the screen's opalescence silvered his hair and misted the outlines of his jaw, giving him an aspect of senility.

"Well, young man," Forrester growled. "What is it? What do you want?"

The irritation in the captain's voice seemed to increase Caldwell's agitation. Lawton had to say: "All right, lad, let's have it," before the information which he had seemed bursting to impart could be wrenched out of him.

It came in erratic spurts. "The bubble is all blooming, sir. All around inside there are big yellow and purple growths. It started up above, and—and spread around. First there was just a clouding over of the sky, sir, and then—stalks shot out."

For a moment Lawton felt as though all sanity had been squeezed from his brain. Twice he started to ask a question and thought better of it.

Pumpings were superfluous when he could confirm Caldwell's statement in half a minute for himself. If Caldwell had cracked up—

Caldwell hadn't cracked. When Lawton walked to the quartz port and stared down all the blood drained from his face.

The vegetation was luxuriant, and unearthly. Floating in the sky were serpentine tendrils as thick as a man's wrist, purplish flowers and ropy fungus growths. They twisted and writhed and shot out in all directions, creating a tangle immediately beneath him and curving up toward the ship amidst a welter of seed pods.

He could see the seeds dropping—dropping from pods which reminded him of the darkly horned skate egg sheaths which he had collected in his boyhood from sea beaches at ebb tide.

It was the *unwholesomeness* of the vegetation which chiefly unnerved him. It looked dank, malarial. There were decaying patches on the fungus growths and a miasmal mist was descending from it toward the ship.

The control room was completely still when he turned from the quartz port to meet Forrester's startled gaze.

"Dave, what does it mean?" The question burst explosively from the captain's lips.

"It means—life has appeared and evolved and grown rotten ripe inside the bubble, sir. All in the space of an hour or so."

"But that's—*impossible*."

Lawton shook his head. "It isn't at all, sir. We've had it drummed into us that evolution proceeds at a snailish pace, but what proof have we that it can't mutate with lightning-like rapidity? I've told you there are gases outside we can't even make in a chemical laboratory, molecular arrangements that are alien to earth."

"But plants derive nourishment from the soil," interpolated Forrester.

"I know. But if there are alien gases in the air the surface of the bubble must be reeking with unheard of chemicals. There may be compounds inside the bubble which have so sped up organic processes that a hundred million year cycle of mutations has been telescoped into an hour."

Lawton was pacing the floor again. "It would be simpler to assume that seeds of existing plants became somehow caught up and imprisoned in the bubble. But the plants around us never existed on earth. I'm no botanist, but I know what the Congo has on tap, and the great rain forests of the Amazon."

"Dave, if the growth continues it will fill the bubble. It will choke off all our air."

"Don't you suppose I realize that? We've got to destroy that growth before it destroys us."

It was pitiful to watch the crew's morale sag. The miasmal taint of the ominously proliferating vegetation was soon pervading the ship, spreading demoralization everywhere.

It was particularly awful straight down. Above a ropy tangle of livid vines and creepers a kingly stench weed towered, purplish and bloated and weighted down with seed pods.

It seemed sentient, somehow. It was growing so fast that the evil odor which poured from it could be correlated with the increase of tension inside the ship. From that particular plant, minute by slow minute, there surged a continuously mounting offensiveness, like nothing Lawton had ever smelt before.

The bubble had become a blooming horror sailing slowly westward above the storm-tossed Atlantic. And all the chemical agents which Lawton sprayed through the ventilation valves failed to impede the growth or destroy a single seed pod.

It was difficult to kill plant life with chemicals which were not harmful to man. Lawton took dangerous risks, increasing the unwholesomeness of their rapidly dwindling air supply by spraying out a thin diffusion of problematically poisonous acids.

It was no sale. The growths increased by leaps and bounds, as though determined to show their resentment of the measures taken against them by marshalling all their forces in a demoralizing plantkrieg.

Thwarted, desperate, Lawton played his last card. He sent five members of the crew, equipped with blow guns. They returned screaming. Lawton had to fortify himself with a double whiskey soda before he could face the look of reproach in their eyes long enough to get all of the prickles out of them.

From then on pandemonium reigned. Blue funk seized the petty officers while some of the crew ran amuck. One member of the engine watch attacked four of his companions with a wrench; another went into the ship's kitchen and slashed himself with a paring knife. The assistant engineer leapt through a 'chute opening, after avowing that he preferred impalement to suffocation.

He *was* impaled. It was horrible. Looking down, Lawton could see his twisted body dangling on a crimson-stippled thorn-like growth forty feet in height.

Slashaway was standing at his elbow in that Waterloo moment, his rough-hewn features twitching. "I can't stand it, sir. It's driving me squirrelly."

"I know, Slashaway. There's something worse than marijuana weed down there."

Slashaway swallowed hard. "That poor guy down there did the wise thing."

Lawton husked: "Stamp on that idea, Slashaway—kill it. We're stronger than he was. There isn't an ounce of weakness in us. We've got what it takes."

"A guy can stand just so much."

"Bosh. There's no limit to what a man can stand."

From the visiplate behind them came an urgent voice: "Radio room tuning in, sir."

Lawton swung about. On the flickering screen the foggy outlines of a face appeared and coalesced into sharpness.

The Perseus radio operator was breathless with excitement. "Our reception is improving, sir. European short waves are coming in strong. The static is terrific, but we're getting every station on the continent, and most of the American stations."

Lawton's eyes narrowed to exultant slits. He spat on the deck, a slow tremor shaking him.

"Slashaway, did you hear that? *We've done it.* We've won against hell and high water."

"We done what, sir?"

"The bubble, you ape—it must be wearing thin. Hell's bells, do you have to stand there gaping like a moronic ninepin? I tell you, we've got it licked."

"I can't stand it, sir. I'm going nuts."

"No you're not. You're slugging the thing inside you that wants to quit. Slashaway, I'm going to give the crew a first-class pep talk. There'll be no stampeding while I'm in command here."

He turned to the radio operator. "Tune in the control room. Tell the captain I want every member of the crew lined up on this screen immediately."

The face in the visiplate paled. "I can't do that, sir. Ship's regulations—"

Lawton transfixed the operator with an irate stare. "The captain told you to report directly to me, didn't he?"

"Yes sir, but—"

"If you don't want to be cashiered, *snap into it.*"

"Yes—yessir."

The captain's startled face preceded the duty-muster visiview by a full minute, seeming to project outward from the screen. The veins on his neck were thick blue cords.

"Dave," he croaked. "Are you out of your mind? What good will talking do *now*?"

"Are the men lined up?" Lawton rapped, impatiently.

Forrester nodded. "They're all in the engine room, Dave."

"Good. Block them in."

The captain's face receded, and a scene of tragic horror filled the opalescent visiplate. The men were not standing at attention at all. They were slumping against the Perseus' central charging plant in attitudes of abject despair.

Madness burned in the eyes of three or four of them. Others had torn open their shirts, and raked their flesh with their nails. Petty officer Caldwell was standing as straight as a totem pole, clenching and unclenching his hands. The second assistant engineer was sticking out his tongue. His face was deadpan, which made what was obviously a terror reflex look like an idiot's grimace.

Lawton moistened his lips. "Men, listen to me. There is some sort of plant outside that is giving off deliriant fumes. A few of us seem to be immune to it.

"I'm not immune, but I'm fighting it, and all of you boys can fight it too. I want you to fight it to the top of your courage. You can fight *anything* when you know that just around the corner is freedom from a beastliness that deserves to be licked—even if it's only a plant.

"Men, we're blasting our way free. The bubble's wearing thin. Any minute now the plants beneath us may fall with a soggy plop into the Atlantic Ocean.

"I want every man jack aboard this ship to stand at his post and obey orders. Right this minute you look like something the cat dragged in. But most men who cover themselves with glory start off looking even worse than you do."

He smiled wryly.

"I guess that's all. I've never had to make a speech in my life, and I'd hate like hell to start now."

It was petty officer Caldwell who started the chant. He started it, and the men took it up until it was coming from all of them in a full-throated roar.

> *I'm a tough, true-hearted skyman,*
>   *Careless and all that, d'ye see?*
> *Never at fate a railer,*
>   *What is time or tide to me?*
>
> *All must die when fate shall will it,*
>   *I can never die but once,*
> *I'm a tough, true-hearted skyman;*
>   *He who fears death is a dunce.*

Lawton squared his shoulders. With a crew like that nothing could stop him! Ah, his energies were surging high. The deliriant weed held no terrors for him now. They were stout-hearted lads and he'd go to hell with them cheerfully, if need be.

It wasn't easy to wait. The next half hour was filled with a steadily mounting tension as Lawton moved like a young tornado about the ship, issuing orders and seeing that each man was at his post.

"Steady, Jimmy. The way to fight a deliriant is to keep your mind on a set task. Keep sweating, lad."

"Harry, that winch needs tightening. We can't afford to miss a trick."

"Yeah, it will come suddenly. We've got to get the rotaries started the instant the bottom drops out."

He was with the captain and Slashaway in the control room when it came. There was a sudden, grinding jolt, and the captain's desk started moving toward the quartz port, carrying Lawton with it.

"Holy Jiminy cricket," exclaimed Slashaway.

The deck tilted sharply; then righted itself. A sudden gush of clear, cold air came through the ventilation valves as the triple rotaries started up with a roar.

Lawton and the captain reached the quartz port simultaneously. Shoulder to shoulder they stood staring down at the storm-tossed Atlantic, electrified by what they saw.

Floating on the waves far beneath them was an undulating mass of vegetation, its surface flecked with glinting foam. As it rose and fell in waning sunlight a tainted seepage spread about it, defiling the clean surface of the sea.

But it wasn't the floating mass which drew a gasp from Forrester, and caused Lawton's scalp to prickle. Crawling slowly across that Sargasso-like island of noxious vegetation was a huge, elongated shape which bore a nauseous resemblance to a mottled garden slug.

Forrester was trembling visibly when he turned from the quartz port.

"God, Dave, that would have been the *last straw*. Animal life. Dave, I—I can't realize we're actually out of it."

"We're out, all right," Lawton said, hoarsely. "Just in time, too. Skipper, you'd better issue grog all around. The men will be needing it. I'm taking mine straight. You've accused me of being primitive. Wait till you see me an hour from now."

Dr. Stephen Halday stood in the door of his Appalachian mountain laboratory staring out into the pine-scented dusk, a worried expression on his bland, small-featured face. It had happened again. A portion of his experiment had soared skyward, in a very loose group of highly energized wavicles. He wondered if it wouldn't form a sort of sub-electronic macrocosm high in the stratosphere, altering even the air and dust particles which had spurted up with it, its uncharged atomic particles combining with hydrogen and creating new molecular arrangements.

If such were the case there would be eight of them now. *His* bubbles, floating through the sky. They couldn't possibly harm anything—way up there in the stratosphere. But he felt a little uneasy about it all the same. He'd have to be more careful in the future, he told himself. Much more careful. He didn't want the Controllers to turn back the clock of civilization a century by stopping all atom-smashing experiments.

THE MISSISSIPPI SAUCER

Jimmy watched the *Natchez Belle* draw near, a shining eagerness in his stare. He stood on the deck of the shantyboat, his toes sticking out of his socks, his heart knocking against his ribs. Straight down the river the big packet boat came, purpling the water with its shadow, its smokestacks belching soot.

Jimmy had a wild talent for collecting things. He knew exactly how to infuriate the captains without sticking out his neck. Up and down the Father of Waters, from the bayous of Louisiana to the Great Sandy other little shantyboat boys envied Jimmy and tried hard to imitate him.

But Jimmy had a very special gift, a genius for pantomime. He'd wait until there was a glimmer of red flame on the river and small objects stood out with a startling clarity. Then he'd go into his act.

Nothing upset the captains quite so much as Jimmy's habit of holding a big, croaking bullfrog up by its legs as the riverboats went steaming past. It was a surefire way of reminding the captains that men and frogs were brothers under the skin. The puffed-out throat of the frog told the captains exactly what Jimmy thought of their cheek.

Jimmy refrained from making faces, or sticking out his tongue at the grinning roustabouts. It was the frog that did the trick.

In the still dawn things came sailing Jimmy's way, hurled by captains with a twinkle of repressed merriment dancing in eyes that were kindlier and more tolerant than Jimmy dreamed.

Just because shantyboat folk had no right to insult the riverboats Jimmy had collected forty empty tobacco tins, a down-at-heels shoe, a Sears Roebuck catalogue and—more rolled up newspapers than Jimmy could ever read.

Jimmy could read, of course. No matter how badly Uncle Al needed a new pair of shoes, Jimmy's education came first. So Jimmy had spent six winters ashore in a first-class grammar school, his books paid for out of Uncle Al's "New Orleans" money.

Uncle Al, blowing on a vinegar jug and making sweet music, the holes in his socks much bigger than the holes in Jimmy's socks.

Uncle Al shaking his head and saying sadly, "Some day, young fella, I ain't gonna sit here harmonizing. No siree! I'm gonna buy myself a brand new store suit, trade in this here jig jug for a big round banjo, and hie myself off to the Mardi Gras. Ain't too old thataway to git a little fun out of life, young fella!"

Poor old Uncle Al. The money he'd saved up for the Mardi Gras never seemed to stretch far enough. There was enough kindness in him to stretch like a rainbow over the bayous and the river forests of sweet, rustling pine for as far as the eye could see. Enough kindness to wrap all of Jimmy's life in a glow, and the life of Jimmy's sister as well.

Jimmy's parents had died of winter pneumonia too soon to appreciate Uncle Al. But up and down the river everyone knew that Uncle Al was a great man.

E nemies? Well, sure, all great men made enemies, didn't they? The Harmon brothers were downright sinful about carrying their feuding meanness right up to the doorstep of Uncle Al, if it could be said that a man living in a shantyboat had a doorstep.

Uncle Al made big catches and the Harmon brothers never seemed to have any luck. So, long before Jimmy was old enough to understand how corrosive envy could be the Harmon brothers had started feuding with Uncle Al.

"Jimmy, here comes the *Natchez Belle*! Uncle Al says for you to get him a newspaper. The newspaper you got him yesterday he couldn't read no-ways. It was soaking wet!"

Jimmy turned to glower at his sister. Up and down the river Pigtail Anne was known as a tomboy, but she wasn't—no-ways. She was Jimmy's little sister. That meant Jimmy was the man in the family, and wore the pants, and nothing Pigtail said or did could change that for one minute.

"Don't yell at me!" Jimmy complained. "How can I get Captain Simmons mad if you get me mad first? Have a heart, will you?"

But Pigtail Anne refused to budge. Even when the *Natchez Belle* loomed so close to the shantyboat that it blotted out the sky she continued to crowd her brother, preventing him from holding up the frog and making Captain Simmons squirm.

But Jimmy got the newspaper anyway. Captain Simmons had

a keen insight into tomboy psychology, and from the bridge of the *Natchez Belle* he could see that Pigtail was making life miserable for Jimmy.

True—Jimmy had no respect for packet boats and deserved a good trouncing. But what a scrapper the lad was! Never let it be said that in a struggle between the sexes the men of the river did not stand shoulder to shoulder.

The paper came sailing over the shining brown water like a white-bellied buffalo cat shot from a sling.

Pigtail grabbed it before Jimmy could give her a shove. Calmly she unwrapped it, her chin tilted in bellicose defiance.

As the *Natchez Belle* dwindled around a lazy, cypress-shadowed bend Pigtail Anne became a superior being, wrapped in a cosmopolitan aura. A wide-eyed little girl on a swaying deck, the great outside world rushing straight toward her from all directions.

Pigtail could take that world in her stride. She liked the fashion page best, but she was not above clicking her tongue at everything in the paper.

"Kidnap plot linked to airliner crash killing fifty," she read. "Red Sox blank Yanks! Congress sits today, vowing vengeance! Million dollar heiress elopes with a clerk! Court lets dog pick owner! Girl of eight kills her brother in accidental shooting!"

"I ought to push your face right down in the mud," Jimmy muttered.

"Don't you dare! I've a right to see what's going on in the world!"

"You said the paper was for Uncle Al!"

"It is—when I get finished with it."

Jimmy started to take hold of his sister's wrist and pry the paper from her clasp. Only started—for as Pigtail wriggled back sunlight fell on a shadowed part of the paper which drew Jimmy's gaze as sunlight draws dew.

Exciting wasn't the word for the headline. It seemed to blaze out of the page at Jimmy as he stared, his chin nudging Pigtail's shoulder.

NEW FLYING MONSTER REPORTED
BLAZING GULF STATE SKIES

Jimmy snatched the paper and backed away from Pigtail, his eyes glued to the headline. To Jimmy, it seemed more like a dazzling burst of light in the sky.

He was kind to his sister, however. He read the news item aloud, if an account so startling could be called an item:

A New Orleans resident reported today that he saw a big bright object "roundish like a disk" flying north, against the wind. "It was all lighted up from inside!" the observer stated. "As far as I could tell there were no signs of life aboard the thing. It was much bigger than any of the flying saucers previously reported!"

"People keep seeing them!" Jimmy muttered, after a pause. "Nobody knows where they come from! Saucers flying through the sky, high up at night. In the daytime, too! Maybe we're being *watched*, Pigtail!"

"Watched? Jimmy, what do you mean? What you talking about?"

Jimmy stared at his sister, the paper jiggling in his clasp. "It's way over your head, Pigtail!" he said sympathetically. "I'll prove it! What's a planet?"

"A star in the sky, you dope!" Pigtail almost screamed. "Wait'll Uncle Al hears what a meanie you are. If I wasn't your sister you wouldn't dare grab a paper that doesn't belong to you."

Jimmy refused to be enraged. "A planet's not a star, Pigtail," he said patiently. "A star's a big ball of fire like the sun. A planet is small and cool, like the Earth. Some of the planets may even have people on them. Not people like us, but people all the same. Maybe we're just frogs to them!"

"You're crazy, Jimmy! Crazy, crazy, you hear?"

Jimmy started to reply, then shut his mouth tight. Big waves were nothing new in the wake of steamboats, but the shantyboat wasn't just riding a swell. It was swaying and rocking like a floating barrel in the kind of blow Shantyboaters dreaded worse than the thought of dying.

Jimmy knew that a big blow could come up fast. Straight down from the sky in gusts, from all directions, banging against the boat like a drunken roustabout, slamming doors, tearing away mooring planks.

The river could rise fast too. Under the lashing of a hurricane blowing up from the gulf the river could lift a shantyboat right out of the water, and smash it to smithereens against a tree.

But now the blow was coming from just one part of the sky. A funnel of wind was churning the river into a white froth and raising big swells directly offshore. But the river wasn't rising and the sun was shining in a clear sky.

Jimmy knew a dangerous floodwater storm when he saw one. The sky had to be dark with rain, and you had to feel scared, in fear of drowning.

Jimmy was scared, all right. That part of it rang true. But a hollow, sick feeling in his chest couldn't mean anything by itself, he told himself fiercely.

Pigtail Anne saw the disk before Jimmy did. She screamed and pointed skyward, her twin braids standing straight out in the wind like the ropes on a bale of cotton, when smokestacks collapse and a savage howling sends the river ghosts scurrying for cover.

Straight down out of the sky the disk swooped, a huge, spinning shape as flat as a buckwheat cake swimming in a golden haze of butterfat.

But the disk didn't remind Jimmy of a buckwheat cake. It made him think instead of a slowly turning wheel in the pilot house of a rotting old riverboat, a big, ghostly wheel manned by a steersman a century dead, his eye sockets filled with flickering swamp lights.

It made Jimmy want to run and hide. Almost it made him want to cling to his sister, content to let her wear the pants if only he could be spared the horror.

For there was something so chilling about the downsweeping disk that Jimmy's heart began leaping like a vinegar jug bobbing about in the wake of a capsizing fishboat.

Lower and lower the disk swept, trailing plumes of white smoke, lashing the water with a fearful blow. Straight down over the cypress wilderness that fringed the opposite bank, and then out across the river with a long-drawn whistling sound, louder than the air-sucking death gasps of a thousand buffalo cats.

Jimmy didn't see the disk strike the shining broad shoulders of the Father of Waters, for the bend around which the *Natchez Belle* had steamed so proudly hid the sky monster from view. But Jimmy did see the waterspout, spiraling skyward like the atom bomb explosion he'd goggled at in the pages of an old *Life* magazine, all smudged now with oily thumbprints.

Just a roaring for an instant—and a big white mushroom shooting straight up into the sky. Then, slowly, the mushroom decayed and fell back, and an awful stillness settled down over the river.

The stillness was broken by a shrill cry from Pigtail Anne. "It was a flying saucer! Jimmy, we've seen one! We've seen one! We've—"

"Shut your mouth, Pigtail!"

Jimmy shaded his eyes and stared out across the river, his chest a throbbing ache.

He was still staring when a door creaked behind him.

Jimmy trembled. A tingling fear went through him, for he found it hard to realize that the disk had swept around the bend out of sight. To his overheated imagination it continued to fill all of the sky above him, overshadowing the shantyboat, making every sound a threat.

Sucking the still air deep into his lungs, Jimmy swung about.

Uncle Al was standing on the deck in a little pool of sunlight, his gaunt, hollow-cheeked face set in harsh lines. Uncle Al was shading his eyes too. But he was staring up the river, not down.

"Trouble, young fella," he grunted. "Sure as I'm a-standin' here. A barrelful o' trouble—headin' straight for us!"

Jimmy gulped and gestured wildly toward the bend. "It came down *over there*, Uncle Al!" he got out. "Pigtail saw it, too! A big, flying—"

"The Harmons are a-comin', young fella," Uncle Al drawled, silencing Jimmy with a wave of his hand. "Yesterday I rowed over a Harmon jug line without meanin' to. Now Jed Harmon's tellin' everybody I stole his fish!"

Very calmly Uncle Al cut himself a slice of the strongest tobacco on the river and packed it carefully in his pipe, wadding it down with his thumb.

He started to put the pipe between his teeth, then thought better of it.

"I can bone-feel the Harmon boat a-comin', young fella," he said, using the pipe to gesture with. "Smooth and quiet over the river like a moccasin snake."

Jimmy turned pale. He forgot about the disk and the mushrooming water spout. When he shut his eyes he saw only a red haze overhanging the river, and a shantyboat nosing out of the cypresses, its windows spitting death.

Jimmy knew that the Harmons had waited a long time for an excuse. The Harmons were law-respecting river rats with sharp teeth. Feuding wasn't lawful, but murder could be made lawful by whittling down a lie until it looked as sharp as the truth.

The Harmon brothers would do their whittling down with double-barreled shotguns. It was easy enough to make murder look like a lawful crime if you could point to a body covered by a blanket and say, "We caught him stealing our fish! He was a-goin' to kill us—so we got him first."

No one would think of lifting the blanket and asking Uncle Al about it. A man lying stiff and still under a blanket could no more make himself heard than a river cat frozen in the ice.

"Git inside, young 'uns. *Here they come!*"

Jimmy's heart skipped a beat. Down the river in the sunlight a shantyboat was drifting. Jimmy could see the Harmon brothers crouching on the deck, their faces livid with hate, sunlight glinting on their arm-cradled shotguns.

The Harmon brothers were not in the least alike. Jed Harmon was tall and gaunt, his right cheek puckered by a knife scar, his cruel, thin-lipped mouth snagged by his teeth. Joe Harmon was small and stout, a little round man with bushy eyebrows and the flabby face of a cottonmouth snake.

"Go inside, Pigtail," Jimmy said, calmly. "I'm a-going to stay and fight!"

Uncle Al grabbed Jimmy's arm and swung him around. "You heard what I said, young fella. Now git!"

"I want to stay here and fight with you, Uncle Al," Jimmy said.

"Have you got a gun? Do you want to be blown apart, young fella?"

"I'm not scared, Uncle Al," Jimmy pleaded. "You might get wounded. I know how to shoot straight, Uncle Al. If you get hurt I'll go right on fighting!"

"No you won't, young fella! Take Pigtail inside. You hear me? You want me to take you across my knee and beat the livin' stuffings out of you?"

Silence.

Deep in his uncle's face Jimmy saw an anger he couldn't buck.

Grabbing Pigtail Anne by the arm, he propelled her across the deck and into the dismal front room of the shantyboat.

The instant he released her she glared at him and stamped her foot. "If Uncle Al gets shot it'll be your fault," she said cruelly. Then Pigtail's anger really flared up.

"The Harmons wouldn't dare shoot us 'cause we're children!"

For an instant brief as a dropped heartbeat Jimmy stared at his sister with unconcealed admiration.

"You can be right smart when you've got nothing else on your mind, Pigtail," he said. "If they kill me they'll hang sure as shooting!"

Jimmy was out in the sunlight again before Pigtail could make a grab for him.

Out on the deck and running along the deck toward Uncle Al. He was still running when the first blast came.

It didn't sound like a shotgun blast. The deck shook and a big swirl of smoke floated straight toward Jimmy, half blinding him and blotting Uncle Al from view.

When the smoke cleared, Jimmy could see the Harmon shantyboat. It was less than thirty feet away now, drifting straight past and rocking with the tide like a topheavy flatbarge.

On the deck Jed Harmon was crouching down, his gaunt face split in a triumphant smirk. Beside him Joe Harmon stood quivering like a mound of jelly, a stick of dynamite in his hand, his flabby face looking almost gentle in the slanting sunlight.

There was a little square box at Jed Harmon's feet. As Joe pitched Jed reached into the box for another dynamite stick. Jed was passing the sticks along to his brother, depending on wad dynamite to silence Uncle Al forever.

Wildly Jimmy told himself that the guns had been just a trick to mix Uncle Al up, and keep him from shooting until they had him where they wanted him.

Uncle Al was shooting now, his face as grim as death. His big heavy gun was leaping about like mad, almost hurling him to the deck.

Jimmy saw the second dynamite stick spinning through the

air, but he never saw it come down. All he could see was the smoke and the shantyboat rocking, and another terrible splintering crash as he went plunging into the river from the end of a rising plank, a sob strangling in his throat.

Jimmy struggled up from the river with the long leg-thrusts of a terrified bullfrog, his head a throbbing ache. As he swam shoreward he could see the cypresses on the opposite bank, dark against the sun, and something that looked like the roof of a house with water washing over it.

Then, with mud sucking at his heels, Jimmy was clinging to a slippery bank and staring out across the river, shading his eyes against the glare.

Jimmy thought, "I'm dreaming! I'll wake up and see Uncle Joe blowing on a vinegar jug. I'll see Pigtail, too. Uncle Al will be sitting on the deck, taking it easy!"

But Uncle Al wasn't sitting on the deck. There was no deck for Uncle Al to sit upon. Just the top of the shantyboat, sinking lower and lower, and Uncle Al swimming.

Uncle Al had his arm around Pigtail, and Jimmy could see Pigtail's white face bobbing up and down as Uncle Al breasted the tide with his strong right arm.

Closer to the bend was the Harmon shantyboat. The Harmons were using their shotguns now, blasting fiercely away at Uncle Al and Pigtail. Jimmy could see the smoke curling up from the leaping guns and the water jumping up and down in little spurts all about Uncle Al.

There was an awful hollow agony in Jimmy's chest as he stared, a fear that was partly a soundless screaming and partly a vision of Uncle Al sinking down through the dark water and turning it red.

It was strange, though. Something was happening to Jimmy, nibbling away at the outer edges of the fear like a big, hungry river cat. Making the fear seem less swollen and awful, shredding it away in little flakes.

There was a white core of anger in Jimmy which seemed suddenly to blaze up.

He shut his eyes tight.

In his mind's gaze Jimmy saw himself holding the Harmon brothers up by their long, mottled legs. The Harmon brothers were frogs. Not friendly, good natured frogs like Uncle Al, but snake frogs. Cottonmouth frogs.

All flannel red were their mouths, and they had long evil fangs which dripped poison in the sunlight. But Jimmy wasn't afraid of them no-ways. Not any more. He had too firm a grip on their legs.

"Don't let anything happen to Uncle Al and Pigtail!" Jimmy whispered, as though he were talking to himself. No—not exactly to himself. To someone like himself, only larger. Very close to Jimmy, but larger, more powerful.

"Catch them before they harm Uncle Al! Hurry! *Hurry*!"

There was a strange lifting sensation in Jimmy's chest now. As though he could shake the river if he tried hard enough, tilt it, send it swirling in great thunderous white surges clear down to Lake Pontchartrain.

But Jimmy didn't want to tilt the river. Not with Uncle Al on it and Pigtail, and all those people in New Orleans who would disappear right off the streets. They were frogs too, maybe, but good frogs. Not like the Harmon brothers.

Jimmy had a funny picture of himself much younger than he was. Jimmy saw himself as a great husky baby, standing in the middle of the river and blowing on it with all his might. The waves rose and rose, and Jimmy's cheeks swelled out and the river kept getting angrier.

No—he must fight that.

"Save Uncle Al!" he whispered fiercely. "Just save him—and Pigtail!"

It began to happen the instant Jimmy opened his eyes. Around the bend in the sunlight came a great spinning disk, wrapped in a fiery glow.

Straight toward the Harmon shantyboat the disk swept, water spurting up all about it, its bottom fifty feet wide. There was no collision. Only a brightness for one awful instant where the shantyboat was twisting and turning in the current, a brightness that outshone the rising sun.

Just like a camera flashbulb going off, but bigger, brighter. So big and bright that Jimmy could see the faces of the Harmon brothers fifty times as large as life, shriveling and disappearing in a magnifying burst of flame high above the cypress trees. Just as though a giant in the sky had trained a big burning glass on the Harmon brothers and whipped it back quick.

Whipped it straight up, so that the faces would grow huge

before dissolving as a warning to all snakes. There was an evil anguish in the dissolving faces which made Jimmy's blood run cold. Then the disk was alone in the middle of the river, spinning around and around, the shantyboat swallowed up.

And Uncle Al was still swimming, fearfully close to it.

The net came swirling out of the disk over Uncle Al like a great, dew-drenched gossamer web. It enmeshed him as he swam, so gently that he hardly seemed to struggle or even to be aware of what was happening to him.

Pigtail didn't resist, either. She simply stopped thrashing in Uncle Al's arms, as though a great wonder had come upon her.

Slowly Uncle Al and Pigtail were drawn into the disk. Jimmy could see Uncle Al reclining in the web, with Pigtail in the crook of his arm, his long, angular body as quiet as a butterfly in its deep winter sleep inside a swaying glass cocoon.

Uncle Al and Pigtail, being drawn together into the disk as Jimmy stared, a dull pounding in his chest. After a moment the pounding subsided and a silence settled down over the river.

Jimmy sucked in his breath. The voices began quietly, as though they had been waiting for a long time to speak to Jimmy deep inside his head, and didn't want to frighten him in any way.

"Take it easy, Jimmy! Stay where you are. We're just going to have a friendly little talk with Uncle Al."

"A t-talk?" Jimmy heard himself stammering.

"We knew we'd find you where life flows simply and serenely, Jimmy. Your parents took care of that before they left you with Uncle Al.

"You see, Jimmy, we wanted you to study the Earth people on a great, wide flowing river, far from the cruel, twisted places. To grow up with them, Jimmy—and to understand them. Especially the Uncle Als. For Uncle Al is unspoiled, Jimmy. If there's any hope at all for Earth as we guide and watch it, that hope burns most brightly in the Uncle Als!"

The voice paused, then went on quickly. "You see, Jimmy, you're not human in the same way that your sister is human—or Uncle Al. But you're still young enough to feel human, and we want you to feel human, Jimmy."

"W—Who are you?" Jimmy gasped.

"We are the Shining Ones, Jimmy! For wide wastes of years we have cruised Earth's skies, almost unnoticed by the Earth people.

When darkness wraps the Earth in a great, spinning shroud we hide our ships close to the cities, and glide through the silent streets in search of our young. You see, Jimmy, we must watch and protect the young of our race until sturdiness comes upon them, and they are ready for the Great Change."

For an instant there was a strange, humming sound deep inside Jimmy's head, like the drowsy murmur of bees in a dew-drenched clover patch. Then the voice droned on. "The Earth people are frightened by our ships now, for their cruel wars have put a great fear of death in their hearts. They watch the skies with sharper eyes, and their minds have groped closer to the truth.

"To the Earth people our ships are no longer the fireballs of mysterious legend, haunted will-o'-the-wisps, marsh flickerings and the even more illusive distortions of the sick in mind. It is a long bold step from fireballs to flying saucers, Jimmy. A day will come when the Earth people will be wise enough to put aside fear. Then we can show ourselves to them as we really are, and help them openly."

The voice seemed to take more complete possession of Jimmy's thoughts then, growing louder and more eager, echoing through his mind with the persuasiveness of muted chimes.

"Jimmy, close your eyes tight. We're going to take you across wide gulfs of space to the bright and shining land of your birth."

Jimmy obeyed.

It was a city, and yet it wasn't like New York or Chicago or any of the other cities Jimmy had seen illustrations of in the newspapers and picture magazines.

The buildings were white and domed and shining, and they seemed to tower straight up into the sky. There were streets, too, weaving in and out between the domes like rainbow-colored spider webs in a forest of mushrooms.

There were no people in the city, but down the aerial streets shining objects swirled with the swift easy gliding of flat stones skimming an edge of running water.

Then as Jimmy stared into the depths of the strange glow behind his eyelids the city dwindled and fell away, and he saw a huge circular disk looming in a wilderness of shadows. Straight toward the disk a shining object moved, bearing aloft on filaments of flame a much smaller object that struggled and mewed and reached out little white arms.

Closer and closer the shining object came, until Jimmy could see that it was carrying a human infant that stared straight at Jimmy out of wide, dark eyes. But before he could get a really good look at the shining object it pierced the shadows and passed into the disk.

There was a sudden, blinding burst of light, and the disk was gone.

Jimmy opened his eyes.

"You were once like that baby, Jimmy!" the voice said. "You were carried by your parents into a waiting ship, and then out across wide gulfs of space to Earth.

"You see, Jimmy, our race was once entirely human. But as we grew to maturity we left the warm little worlds where our infancy was spent, and boldly sought the stars, shedding our humanness as sunlight sheds the dew, or a bright, soaring moth of the night its ugly pupa case.

"We grew great and wise, Jimmy, but not quite wise enough to shed our human heritage of love and joy and heartbreak. In our childhood we must return to the scenes of our past, to take root again in familiar soil, to grow in power and wisdom slowly and sturdily, like a seed dropped back into the loam which nourished the great flowering mother plant.

"Or like the eel of Earth's seas, Jimmy, that must be spawned in the depths of the great cold ocean, and swim slowly back to the bright highlands and the shining rivers of Earth. Young eels do not resemble their parents, Jimmy. They're white and thin and transparent and have to struggle hard to survive and grow up.

"Jimmy, you were planted here by your parents to grow wise and strong. Deep in your mind you knew that we had come to seek you out, for we are all born human, and are bound one to another by that knowledge, and that secret trust.

"You knew that we would watch over you and see that no harm would come to you. You called out to us, Jimmy, with all the strength of your mind and heart. Your Uncle Al was in danger and you sensed our nearness.

"It was partly your knowledge that saved him, Jimmy. But it took courage too, and a willingness to believe that you were more than human, and armed with the great proud strength and wisdom of the Shining Ones."

The voice grew suddenly gentle, like a caressing wind.

"You're not old enough yet to go home, Jimmy! Or wise enough. We'll take you home when the time comes. Now we just want to have a talk with Uncle Al, to find out how you're getting along."

Jimmy looked down into the river and then up into the sky. Deep down under the dark, swirling water he could see life taking shape in a thousand forms. Caddis flies building bright, shining new nests, and dragonfly nymphs crawling up toward the sunlight, and pollywogs growing sturdy hindlimbs to conquer the land.

But there were cottonmouths down there too, with death behind their fangs, and no love for the life that was crawling upward. When Jimmy looked up into the sky he could see all the blazing stars of space, with cottonmouths on every planet of every sun.

Uncle Al was like a bright caddis fly building a fine new nest, thatched with kindness, denying himself bright little Mardi Gras pleasures so that Jimmy could go to school and grow wiser than Uncle Al.

"That's right, Jimmy. You're growing up—we can see that! Uncle Al says he told you to bide from the cottonmouths. But you were ready to give your life for your sister and Uncle Al."

"Shucks, it was nothing!" Jimmy heard himself protesting.

"Uncle Al doesn't think so. And neither do we!"

A long silence came while the river mists seemed to weave a bright cocoon of radiance about Jimmy clinging to the bank, and the great circular disk that had swallowed up Uncle Al. Then the voices began again.

"No reason why Uncle Al shouldn't have a little fun out of life, Jimmy. Gold's easy to make and we'll make some right now. A big lump of gold in Uncle Al's hand won't hurt him in any way."

"Whenever he gets any spending money he gives it away!" Jimmy gulped.

"I know, Jimmy. But he'll listen to you. Tell him you want to go to New Orleans, too!"

Jimmy looked up quickly then. In his heart was something of the wonder he'd felt when he'd seen his first riverboat and waited for he knew not what. Something of the wonder that must have come to men seeking magic in the sky, the rainmakers of ancient tribes and of days long vanished.

Only to Jimmy the wonder came now with a white burst of remembrance and recognition.

It was as though he could sense something of himself in the two towering spheres that rose straight up out of the water behind the disk. Still and white and beautiful they were, like bubbles floating on a rainbow sea with all the stars of space behind them.

Staring at them, Jimmy saw himself as he would be, and knew himself for what he was. It was not a glory to be long endured.

"Now you must forget again, Jimmy! Forget as Uncle Al will forget—until we come for you. Be a little shantyboat boy! You are safe on the wide bosom of the Father of Waters. Your parents planted you in a rich and kindly loam, and in all the finite universes you will find no cosier nook, for life flows here with a diversity that is infinite and—*Pigtail*! She gets on your nerves at times, doesn't she, Jimmy?"

"She sure does," Jimmy admitted.

"Be patient with her, Jimmy. She's the only human sister you'll ever have on Earth."

"I—I'll try!" Jimmy muttered.

Uncle Al and Pigtail came out of the disk in an amazingly simple way. They just seemed to float out, in the glimmering web. Then, suddenly, there wasn't any disk on the river at all—just a dull flickering where the sky had opened like a great, blazing furnace to swallow it up.

"I was just swimmin' along with Pigtail, not worryin' too much, 'cause there's no sense in worryin' when death is starin' you in the face," Uncle Al muttered, a few minutes later.

Uncle Al sat on the riverbank beside Jimmy, staring down at his palm, his vision misted a little by a furious blinking.

"It's gold, Uncle Al!" Pigtail shrilled. "A big lump of solid gold—"

"I just felt my hand get heavy and there it was, young fella, nestling there in my palm!"

Jimmy didn't seem to be able to say anything.

"High school books don't cost no more than grammar school books, young fella," Uncle Al said, his face a sudden shining. "Next winter you'll be a-goin' to high school, sure as I'm a-sittin' here!"

For a moment the sunlight seemed to blaze so brightly about Uncle Al that Jimmy couldn't even see the holes in his socks.

Then Uncle Al made a wry face. "Someday, young fella, when your books are all paid for, I'm gonna buy myself a brand new store suit, and hie myself off to the Mardi Gras. Ain't too old thataway to git a little fun out of life, young fella!"